PLAY FAIR WITH LOVE

PLAY FAIR WITH LOVE

Patricia Robins

CHIVERS

| British Library Cataloguing in Publication Data available |

This Large Print edition published by BBC Audiobooks Ltd, Bath, 2010.
Published by arrangement with the Author.

U.K. Hardcover ISBN 978 1 408 45742 9
U.K. Softcover ISBN 978 1 408 45743 6

Copyright © Patricia Robins 1972

Printed and bound in Great Britain by
CPI Antony Rowe, Chippenham and Eastbourne

CHAPTER ONE

'If you would only marry me, Hatty, it would solve everything!'

'I'm sorry, Justin, but I can't . . . and don't call me Hatty; you know I hate it!'

The young man's serious expression softened into a grin.

'Harriet, then! Do be sensible, darling.' The smile gave way to a frown as he stared into the hazel eyes of the girl beside him. She looked nearer nine than nineteen balanced precariously astride the old brick wall, dangling her long slim legs in their scruffy jeans ravelled at the hem above delicate ankles and dusty bare feet.

'If you would only give me one good reason why not!' he said with semi-pathos, semi-irritation.

Harriet's mouth, full, red and soft, tightened into a harder, more determined line. 'You know why not, Justin. If we weren't ready to get married before . . . before Daddy died . . .' her voice trembled . . . 'then it has to be wrong for me to marry you now just as a way out of my problems. I won't . . . and that's all there is to it.'

She jumped lightly down from the wall and linked her arm through Justin's in a way that indicated quite clearly the familiarity of their

1

friendship.

'Come on—let's go and have tea and stop worrying about me. I'll think of something.'

Justin allowed her to lead him towards the beautiful old brick house, warm and sleepy in the July sunshine.

'You keep saying that but what will you do, Hatty? I do wish you'd let me help.'

The girl did not reply. Gently, she disengaged her arm as if the unconscious gesture underlined her determination to remain independent. Her eyes were concentrated fully now upon the house they were nearing. This was her home, more beloved than anything in the world other than the man, her father, who had shared it with her until that terrible day, a month ago, when he had died and left her quite alone. He had been not only parent but friend, companion, confidant, the pivot round which her world revolved. All her achievements, childish though they might have been, were won so that her father would be proud of her, so that she might measure up to his expectations . . . the silver cups she had won at gymkhanas, the O levels and then the A levels and finally a place at university. If he had done everything humanly possible for her all her life, so she in turn had given him everything she had to give.

His death had left a chasm that she knew no other human being could fill—not even Justin whom she loved very much and who loved her.

2

He was kind, loving, her companion from childhood, her tennis partner, dance partner, the recipient of her girlhood passion. She loved him dearly but she never looked up to and adored him the way she had respected the man who had been the very star in her life and now was gone. She knew, despite his silence on the subject, that Justin felt respect should be gone, too; but then Justin did not understand her father the way she did and judged him now as the world would judge a man who died leaving his daughter penniless.

It was not, Harriet knew, as if he had spent money carelessly and lavishly upon himself. The family capital had been spent in keeping up the beautiful old house for her, because it was *her* home where *she* was happy. He'd kept on her horse and paid her school bills and given her a generous personal allowance because he could not bear to see her go without anything. Old Daley, the accountant, had told her so, peering miserably over his rimless spectacles, his gnarled freckled hands lying helplessly over the sheaths of papers with their columns of spidery figures all in red.

'Your father borrowed money from the bank. The manager was his friend, Harriet. He continued to let him increase his overdraft. Your father could not make the house over to you because he needed it as added security to cover his loans. He intended to sell Swallow Grange eventually but not until you married and left home. If you sell the house well, it should cover capital transfer tax but unfortunately there are other creditors—local tradesmen mostly. I'm afraid there is nothing for it, my dear child, than for you to sell the house and we'll pay off as much as we can.'

'And perhaps leave money owing? Money everyone believed my father would repay?'

'There's no other way!'

'There has to be. I'll think of something!' But no matter how late at night she sat pouring over the figures, there was no other way—until Justin suggested she marry him now instead of waiting until they were both qualified and with their degrees.

'Mother and Father say we can do up the coach house and live there until we can buy a house of our own. You can sell Swallow Grange and Father will lend me five thousand pounds to settle whatever debts remain. When we're both earning, we can repay him.'

'They are my debts, not yours, Justin. I can't do it!'

'Your debts would be mine in any event if we were married!'

'I won't marry you just to get out of financial trouble. We agreed it would be wrong to think of marriage before we qualified. You've another year before you get your M.D. and I've done only a year of my psychology. With you in Edinburgh and me in Cardiff, what kind of married life would we have,

4

Justin? Besides, I'm not ready to get married yet.'

Even to her own ears her final remark sounded ambiguous, coming from someone who professed to be in love. If you were in love, it was natural to want to marry, to be even closer, to share your body and heart and mind—to be one. Somehow she just didn't feel that way about Justin although she loved him dearly. They'd grown up knowing they belonged together; that one day when they were old enough they would fall in love and marry. Some time when she was in her teens and Justin had just left school, he had kissed her for the first time as a lover rather than as a friend and from then on they had been what her father liked to call 'sweethearts'.

'Seeing you two sweethearts holding hands reminds me of the days when I was courting your mother, Harry. It makes me very happy to see you and Justin together!'

Harriet had never known her mother who had died at her birth, but she had nevertheless been an integral part of her life through Dad's memories. He'd brought her up 'the way your mother would have wanted', chose the school 'your mother would have chosen'. His approval of Justin was as much because he liked him as because her mother would have thought him 'just the right young man for you, Harry; steady, honest, kind, hard-working. She always liked doctors, too!'

Life had been so easy, trouble free, tension free, carefree. She sailed blindly over the smooth waters with no real thought of the future beyond getting to university and studying psychology.

'You have a wonderful way of handling the younger children, Harriet,' Mrs Agrew, her head mistress, had said perceptively. 'That's one of the reasons you make such a good prefect. You seem to understand even the more difficult ones. Are you interested in children?'

'I like them!' Harriet said. 'I don't think they are difficult if you can make yourself feel what they feel and treat them the way you'd want to be treated if you were one of them.'

'But that isn't so easy as you may think for a lot of people. You need sensitivity, imagination and perception. You have all three. You're intelligent, too. You could go further than nursing if you really wanted, Harriet—become a doctor, for instance.'

From that small conversation, ambition had formed and grown until it had matured into a certainty and she had gained a place at Cardiff University. The future seemed assured—until suddenly without prior illness, her father had had a coronary and died and the secure background to her world had fallen apart.

'Harriet, you've got to marry me. You've just *got* to!'

Justin's voice pulled Harriet back to the

6

present. They had reached the giant copper beech and Justin was backing her against the trunk, imprisoning her by placing an arm on either side of her. His face was very close to hers so that she could see her own reflection in the brilliant blue of his eyes. His hair, eyebrows and eyelashes were quite golden with the sun slanting down through the leaves. He looked like a young Greek god—handsome by any standards and strong, clean, dearly familiar to her. Yet she felt a million miles apart.

'I love you, Harry. You know that. I'll make you happy. Say you'll marry me. I'll take care of you, darling. Trust me!'

His face came nearer and she closed her eyes. As his mouth touched hers, she felt her body slacken, soften towards him and involuntarily her arms went up and round his neck. His breathing quickened and she felt his desire. But within her there was no answering response. It was always this way—Justin needing her and her mind wanting to respond whilst her body remained untouched by the fire she knew should be there.

'I'm nineteen years old and still a virgin!' she thought. 'Maybe I'm frigid!'

But the thought was a familiar one as was the answer to it—she knew that she was not. There would come an awakening—she knew it in every fibre of her being. But Justin had not been able to fan that spark into a flame. The

7

more intense his desire, the greater her withdrawal, no matter how many times her brain told her: 'You love him, you love him, you love him.'

Gently, she eased him away.

'We're only confusing the issue!' she whispered, although there was no one but Justin to hear. 'I want to think clearly, Justin.'

His voice in reply sounded gravelled and hurt.

'If you felt about me as I do about you, you wouldn't have any doubts. I want you, Harry. I want to marry you. I want to make love to you. You say you love me but . . .'

'I know, Justin. Forgive me. I can't help it. I could pretend but you wouldn't want me to do that and I could never cheat with you.'

He turned away angrily.

'I don't think you're really in love with me at all. You're not a schoolgirl any more, you know. I could understand you being shy and reserved and inhibited when you were in your teens. But you're a woman now, Harriet—a grown-up woman, yet you don't have any of the natural responses of a woman. If I didn't know you better, I'd think you were just plain frigid!'

Her face flushed with anger but it was only momentarily. She understood that he was hurt by her rejection and he'd only voiced her own thoughts and fears.

'Justin, I'd like to be able to explain but I

can't. I *do* love you. I always have. I think I always will. There never has been anyone else I thought I loved or could love.'

'Or anyone else you wanted, Harriet? Has no man aroused a few basic sexual desires in that beautiful body of yours?'

'Justin!' Her voice was full of reproach but the denial on her lips lay unspoken. She had all but forgotten the end of term party and that crazy car ride along the coast with Peter Powell. She remembered his name though little else about the dark-haired Welsh boy. He had had too much to drink and so had she. They'd danced and he'd held her much too close and kissed her violently when the lights were dimmed. Surprised, she'd found herself reacting, her body responding in a quite frightening way, where willpower had little control over her senses. She was both excited and nervous, yet she had agreed without argument when he'd suggested a drive, only pretending to herself that she did not know what the invitation really meant.

He'd stopped the car near some sand dunes and without any romantic preludes, had walked her across the beach to a secluded, moonlit patch and pulled her down on top of him.

The following day Harriet had felt ashamed; not because she had succumbed because fortunately she had been in no position to do so. The combination of desire and too much to drink had so reduced her prospective seducer's powers of restraint, he had not been able to wait for her participation. It was all over before he had half undressed her. But the fact remained she would have participated and because the mere thought of having her first sexual experience with a young man she neither knew nor particularly wished to know was so dismaying and humiliating, she had chosen to forget the incident as quickly and completely as she could.

Now Justin had reminded her of the occasion and she felt the hot colour of embarrassment burn her cheeks. What kind of animal passion had moved her when Justin whom she loved could not? The Welsh boy had been so totally different—a little rough, coarse, hard, primitive, the very opposite to all the qualities she had grown up to believe worthy of love and respect; the very opposite to Justin, to her father. Both were kind, gentle, weak with her.

Even now Justin was apologising for having offended her. The trouble with Justin was that he was much *too* nice to her; maybe too good for her.

'Don't let's quarrel!' she said impulsively. 'I'm sure you're right and I'm being stupid but please be patient. Maybe I just need to grow up a bit. Give me a little time, Justin.'

He softened instantly, clasping her hand and holding it against his cheek protectively.

'It was my fault. It's only natural you're still emotionally upset after your father's death. You've been incredibly brave about it all, darling. I admire your courage.'

Had it not been for the faint shrill of the telephone bell reaching them across the lawn as Justin stopped speaking, Harriet's life might have taken a very different road. Justin's gentleness, tolerance and kindness had so touched her that but for the bell, she would have told him she'd changed her mind; that she would marry him after all. But the bell did ring and sighing, Harriet said:

'I suppose I'd better go and answer it. Wait here for me, Justin. I'll bring tea out with me and we'll have it under the tree.'

She ran across the lawn with a curious sense of urgency. The phone call was probably of no importance and yet she had the feeling that if it were to stop ringing before she answered, she would miss something terribly important. When she reached the hall and lifted the receiver, she was too breathless to gasp more than 'Hullo!'

'Is that you, Miss Rothman? It's John Surry of Eastman and Partners. I hope you won't mind my ringing you but Mr Eastman lunched today with Mr Ainslie and learned that you may be selling Swallow Grange. Mr Eastman asked me to ring up and find out whether this was so or not and if so, whether you would be good enough to let us act for you.'

Harriet drew a deep breath.

'I'm afraid Mr Ainslie has jumped the gun!' she said. 'I haven't made up my mind yet about selling. Naturally, if I do I'll let your firm handle the sale.'

'I see! Look, Miss Rothman, may I talk off the record for a minute? I am a very junior partner here and if I'm talking out of turn and Mr Eastman heard of it, I could be in trouble.'

'You can say anything you want!' Harriet said laughing. 'Have you forgotten you used to compete against me in gymkhanas, John?'

'I hadn't forgotten but I thought you had. It's a good ten years ago and though I've seen you in the village from time to time, we don't seem to have met socially. I'd like to say how sorry I am about your father. We all liked and admired him. To tell you the truth, it gave me quite a shock to hear of Swallow Grange being sold.'

'I'm trying to think of a way not to sell it, John. The trouble is I need the money.'

'Which brings me to what I wanted to ask you—off the record. You wouldn't consider letting it, would you, Harriet? We've got someone on our books who has been pestering me for over a month to find him somewhere to live, and the only place remotely answering his requirements is your house. I never dreamed there might be a chance of offering it to him. The point is, I gather the amount of the rent to be paid is of little or no consequence. Our

12

client will pay absolutely anything to get what he wants and he has the money, too. Is it out of the question?'

'I don't know!' Harriet answered truthfully. 'I've never thought about it. It might be possible. I really don't know. How much rent would I ask, John?'

'Well, that hasn't been discussed. All I know is that the cash side is relatively immaterial. Our client wants what he wants and isn't interested in the bill. If you were to let the house furnished, you might easily get away with three hundred pounds a week, perhaps more. I'm only guessing.'

'But that's fantastic. With that sort of money, I could . . .' she broke off, finishing the sentence in her mind; with that sort of money she could pay off the death duties and the creditors in a few years and still end up owning Swallow Grange.

'Well, think about it and let me know, will you? I can arrange for our client to come and see over the house any time at all.'

'He realises we're miles from anywhere? That apart from the doctor's house, there aren't any neighbours? Not everyone would want to be so isolated, especially in winter.'

'Mr Blake knows the house and likes it. I rather gather that if there's any fault it's that it isn't isolated enough. After all, you are only four miles from the village.'

'No cinema, no bingo, no supermarket, not

13

even a Woolworths!'

'That's the way Mr Blake wants it.'

'And Mrs Blake?'

'I don't even know if there is a wife. *If* there is, he hasn't mentioned her. There's a child, though. I gather it's handicapped in some way though he didn't go into details. But it's for the child's health he wants a country place, fresh air, green grass, trees and so on. Well, I'll leave it with you to think over.'

'No! No, don't! I mean, I don't want time to think it over. Mr Blake can come and see the house as soon as he likes. If he wants it, he can make me an offer. Then I'll think about it. Any time that suits him. I've got to reach a decision about the house sooner or later. Maybe this will help me make up my mind.'

The young estate agent rang off, sounding not a little surprised by Harriet's impetuosity. As she walked through to the kitchen to make tea, Harriet found herself just as surprised. She felt as if she might have acted a little crazily and yet she had committed herself to nothing other than giving a permit to view the house. She did not have to let it if she didn't feel like it. She had not burned any boats . . .

Yet as she carried the tea tray down across the lawn to the beech tree where Justin was patiently waiting, she knew that she had somehow extricated herself from a situation that would have been a commitment. If leasing Swallow Grange turned out to be a way of

14

solving her financial problems, there was no pressure on her to marry Justin. She could remain completely independent and still retain possession of the home she loved even if for a number of years someone else was living in it.

Mr Blake! So far a man without face or personality or a Christian name. All she knew of him was that he had a child . . . and that he had money. Not much to go on. Yet these few facts were enough to have aroused her curiosity.

'Sorry to have been so long, Justin,' she apologised as he took the tray from her. 'But it might be important. I think I am going to let Swallow Grange to a wealthy Mr Blake.'

Fifty miles away, the telephone rang in the outer office of a London businessman. The secretary put the call through to her boss without delay.

'This is John Surry, Mr Blake, of Eastman and Partners. I thought you'd like to know that Miss Rothman is interested in the idea of leasing Swallow Grange. She would like a fairly quick decision so if you are still interested, may I suggest you come up one day this week?'

There was a second's pause before the man said:

'I *am* interested and I'll come up tomorrow morning. Please make an appointment for me. And thank you, Mr Surry. If this goes through, I'll see you are personally rewarded.'

As he replaced the receiver, Martin Blake picked up a photograph from his desk and studied it carefully. The woman smiling back at him was young, lovely, her expression tender and maternal, with one smooth cheek laid against the forehead of a child of about one. The baby's face was delicate, sensitive, the resemblance to the woman very strong.

The man's face tightened as if he were trying to keep his emotions well in check. Nevertheless, his voice was rasping as he said softly:

'God Almighty, I'm doing my best for him, June. I'm doing my best.'

He put the photograph down and with his forefinger, touched the child's head.

'Poor little devil. Poor kid!' he said. 'Losing her was even worse for you. You found your own way to escape. But I can't. I've got to live with it—and you.'

With a sudden abrupt gesture he turned the photograph on its face and his body stiffened. He flicked down a switch on the intercom and his voice normal once more, said firmly:

'Cancel all my appointments for tomorrow, Miss Dean. I'll be going up to Westchester for the day. And please phone home and say I won't be back to dinner. Then book me a hired car to drive me up to Westchester. It can pick me up at home at eight-thirty. And, Miss Dean, I want some cash. Say a thousand in tens. I'll want that before I go home tonight.

16

Oh, yes, and bring me any correspondence you have from Eastman and Partners. I think there are a couple of letters in my personal file. Right away, please.'

He lit a cigarette and smoked without moving until his secretary appeared with the letters. When she had left the room, he picked one up and studied it thoughtfully.

. . . in answer to your query, I am afraid there is no likelihood of the house ever coming on the market. It is the property of a retired Colonel whose family have lived there for several generations. He resides there with his daughter and Mr Eastman does not feel that a cash offer would be in the least appropriate as the Colonel is hardly the kind of man to be tempted by money to leave his home. Mr Eastman regrets that he cannot act for you in such a manner but should the house ever come on the market, we will naturally be pleased to inform you . . .

He flicked down the inter-com switch once more and the small bird-like figure of his middle-aged secretary reappeared instantly, her face as always quite expressionless. Despite her spinster-like appearance, she was the perfect secretary with an unfailing memory and an impassivity which suited his temperament very well indeed. She was methodical, punctual and seemed devoted to his service. This latter qualification he attributed to the fact that he paid her very well indeed—far more than she could hope to get elsewhere and with her looks.

'Get on to our usual enquiry agent, Miss Dean. I want a rush job done on a Colonel Rothman, died about a month ago, formerly living at Swallow Grange, Westchester. There must have been a will. I want full details and any other information the agent can elicit in the district on the Colonel and his surviving daughter's financial position. And, Miss Dean, I want the facts by eight-thirty tomorrow.'

He was watching his secretary's face and for once he detected a faintly disapproving tightening of the lines round her mouth. Amused, he said:

'Anything wrong, Miss Dean?'

She flushed and shook her head.

'No, Mr Blake, they're a good firm and reliable.'

'I pay them well enough!'

'Yes.'

Again he detected the barest hint of disapproval—this time in her voice. With a curiosity totally at variance with his usual distant manner he maintained towards his employee, he asked:

'You don't approve of enquiry agents? Yet the information they supply can make the difference between making a deal and losing it. I want to buy the lease of Swallow Grange, Miss Dean, and I mean to do so. It will help me to know beforehand what kind of price will persuade Miss Rothman to let me have it. You think that is ethically wrong?'

The woman hesitated. Mr Blake had never invited her opinion before and she was not sure whether he desired an honest reply from her. Many years ago she had been taught that a good secretary considered the boss was always right. But somehow Mr Blake differed very widely from her previous employers. To begin with, he was not born a gentleman. He was a self-made man and with it, arrogant, dictatorial, proud and as hard as nails. Yet with all, he was fair. He exacted perfection from his staff but as he told them when signing them on, they were well paid in return.

She drew a little breath and said primly but bravely:

'Money isn't everything, Mr Blake.'

To her surprise, he laughed. He was not a man given to humour.

'My dear Miss Dean, if you had come up the hard way as I have, you'd know very well that money is everything when it comes to getting what you want from life. Every man has his price.'

'There is on occasions, the question of principles!' Miss Dean argued stubbornly. 'Some people, Mr Blake, set more store on these than on money.'

He was still smiling, his mouth curved cynically at the edges.

'I disagree. You can buy people's principles, even their morals if you can pay the price. I'm sure *you* are a woman of principle, Miss Dean, yet I venture to suggest even you could be bought.'

She shook her head in denial.

'Come now, let us take a hypothetical example. You would count yourself a woman of convention, of good moral behaviour I am sure. But suppose there was, let us say, a wealthy sheik who was prepared to offer you a thousand pounds if you would agree to spend one night in his harem. Would you refuse, Miss Dean? Of course you would! But suppose he were to offer you fifty thousand pounds? What then?'

'I would still refuse!' she said primly.

'For a quarter of a million, Miss Dean?'

Her hesitation was fractional but Martin Blake saw it.

'Then you would most certainly give in for a million. So you, too, have your price. Have I proved my point?'

Miss Dean's mouth tightened.

'With regard to me, yes. But I still maintain there exist some people who cannot be bought.'

'Then I look forward to meeting one of them one day!' Martin Blake said easily. 'Meanwhile, Miss Dean, I shall continue to do business my way and I trust for both our sakes that I shall continue to flourish.'

But when she left the room, the man's expression changed as once more he looked at the photograph on his desk. Gone were the hard cynical lines about his mouth. The lips looked twisted and bitter and the large dark eyes set wide apart in a tanned, strong face, were softened into liquid pools of misery.

Miss Dean, he told himself wretchedly, was not after all so far from touching on the truth. There were some things, if not some people, that money couldn't buy. Not one of the children's specialists here in England or last summer in the States had been able to cure his son. The best any of them could offer was 'a special boarding school where some progress might be hoped for'. Not one would promise an eventual cure.

He drew a long shuddering breath. For a moment his hunched shoulders and the look of defeat that had captured his face made him appear far older than his thirty-two years. Then his back straightened and the slackened mouth tautened into its customary lines of firmness and decision. For the last time that morning, he pressed the intercom switch.

'Miss Dean I've decided to take the family with me tomorrow. Will you inform them when you make that call to my home. If they have any prior engagements, they must cancel them.'

Then he lent back in his chair and slowly lit a cigarette. Molly wouldn't like being instructed by Miss Dean. On the other hand, he had no wish to become involved in

21

arguments as to why she and Peter could not make the journey to Westchester. He had made up his mind they would go with him and nothing she could say would alter it, so he might as well avoid any discussions that would ensue. To say the least she would be surprised by his sudden decision to leave London for a remote country house miles from civilisation. He'd never talked to her about his plans for Peter, knowing that she would be certain to oppose any move away from the sophisticated life of London and the luxurious comfortable London house where they had lived since his return from America. Nevertheless, he had little doubt that she would ultimately acquiesce. That was one thing he could count on with Molly—she was so devoted both to himself and Peter that she would go with them to the ends of the world rather than be parted from them. She might grumble, but she'd go. And once she saw Swallow Grange, sensed its quiet antique beauty and peacefulness, she would realise for herself how such a place might benefit Peter.

It was strange, Martin told himself, how that house had captured his imagination. Born and brought up in the slums of Birmingham, he was city bred and had no environmental roots in the country. Nonetheless, he felt at home there in the oddest way. He had been driving back to London from a conference when his driver had missed the road, so that they had somehow found their way to Westchester. In order to regain the main road, they had had to drive through the village and out on the south side where, quite suddenly, he had glimpsed the old Queen Anne manor house basking in early spring sunshine, its bricks glowing a pinkish red, half hidden by an immense copper beech tree as yet only in tight bud. An old white pony grazed in the paddock adjoining the unkept gardens. An elderly gardener was pulling grass tufts from the gravelled drive. A young girl sat perched on his wheelbarrow, her hair blowing across her face, obscuring it from his view.

He had instructed his driver to slow the car. There was an air of quiet peace about the house and gardens in which it lay, that contrasted acutely with the steel and concrete city from which he had just driven. This was the kind of small estate he had always felt epitomised the English upper middle classes— the home of the type of people he had wanted to emulate when he was old enough to realise that he could escape from his slum background. He'd seen coloured photographs of houses such as this in glossy magazines and known that one day he would have the kind of money that would enable him to live in one.

A keen intelligence, natural shrewdness and a capacity for enduring long hours of hard work took him moderately quickly up the ladder. He rose from the position of manager of his firm to managing director of the London head office. From there he was sent to America where he consolidated his reputation and met the girl who was to become his wife. She was everything he had set his heart on—pretty, amusing, of excellent family background and very, very rich. He was promoted to director level and bought an apartment in New York and a house in California. With the help of his wife's capital, he bought a controlling interest in the business in which he had begun as office boy. The future was assured. His first son was born and except for occasional twinges of restlessness he could not explain, Martin was perfectly content. Then his wife died, suddenly and horribly in a sailing accident in the Bahamas while they were there on holiday. The shock to Martin was acute but at first seemed to make little impact on their son. His wife's sister, Molly, came to look after the boy and Martin decided to return to England. Six months after the accident, little Peter suddenly became mute. The doctors seemed to think it was delayed shock from which he would soon recover. However, the boy became more and more withdrawn until Martin felt he was losing all contact with the child. He began taking him to the best pediatricians. The evidence that Peter was now 'autistic' began to accumulate. He flew the boy to America where the same diagnosis was given. Martin steadfastly refused to consider a special school.

'He's too young. I won't send him away!'

Had it not been for Molly's devoted care of the boy, he might have had to give in. Now completely detached from the world around him, the child became increasingly difficult to handle and lived in a world of his own, sometimes humming to himself quietly for hours on end, but at others throwing violent tantrums and breaking everything within reach. Martin was well aware that the few friends they had thought it wrong to keep the boy at home, but Molly supported him totally in his desire to keep his little son in an atmosphere where he knew he was loved and cherished. The child was Martin's one weakness and to send him away to live among strangers implied rejection. He convinced himself that given time, Peter would return to normal. As there appeared to be nothing organically wrong, no sign of mental disorder through physical factors, he had succeeded in talking himself into a genuine belief that all that was needed was time, love and care.

London did not appear to have any beneficial effect upon the child. He looked pale, thin and very undersized. Martin had already made up his mind to move into the country before the day he came upon Swallow Grange.

Now, it looked as if the house would be his. In fact, he had no doubt at all that it would.

The unknown Miss Rothman would have her price and he'd pay it. Even colonels' daughters of impeccable pedigree were not averse to money. He could imagine her, either horsey and tweedy or a brainless debutante. Either way it would be a pleasure to best her in the deal.

He buttoned up his jacket and left his office, telling Miss Dean that he would be lunching for the next hour at his favourite pub down the road. At three o'clock he had a conference and at five an appointment with Cynthia—an amusing American divorcee with whom he was currently having a casual affair. She made no emotional demands upon him and the word love was never mentioned. It was very nearly a business arrangement, disguised by expensive dinners and expensive presents. It meant she was available when it suited him and more important, made no effort to pursue him when he chose to stay away from her. She was tactful, amusing and good in bed.

He had not yet made up his mind whether to tell her he was buying the lease of a country house and would be out of town at weekends. He thought he would not bother. There would be time enough to wine and dine her during the week days when his business affairs would necessitate his remaining in London. She would hear the news soon enough from Molly who was a friend of hers—or passed as a friend. If Molly knew he and Cynthia were lovers . . .

With accustomed ease, Martin put this train of thought out of his mind. He had room only for priorities and 'if's and but's' were not facts on which he believed in wasting energy.

CHAPTER TWO

'Mr Eastman was regrettably rather vague on the matter of money,' Martin said as soon as they were all seated in the drawing room and introductions had been made. 'Some people find it difficult to discuss money but as a business man, I do not. May I have your permission, therefore, to come to the point?'

Harriet swept the long strands of hair away from her face in a gesture Justin would have known to be nervous and Martin guessed.

'But you haven't seen the house yet, Mr Blake.'

'I'll see it in a minute. I've no doubt it will suit me. But there is no point wasting your time or mine if we cannot agree on terms. Now, may I suggest that it is quite customary these days to pay what I believe is known as a Deposit. I'm quite willing to do this and I suggest two thousand pounds as a down payment and a weekly rent of three hundred and fifty pounds for three years. I would expect, of course, to be responsible for rates,

27

decorations and other such items.'

He paused, waiting for Harriet to control her incredulous surprise. He concealed his own little smile of triumph. The bait was taken.

'I really don't know, Mr Blake. That seems ... well, to be honest, it seems too much!'

'I don't think my offer is ungenerous. At the same time, may I give you a little advice, Miss Rothman? Never, when you are conducting a deal, let your client know that you think he's paying too much. That's bad business. If it will make you feel any better, I'll confess that had you insisted, I would have gone higher! I like this house. I want to live here.'

Harriet let out her breath. She had told Justin that she did not want him here while she showed her prospective tenants round the house. She felt his disapproval of the whole idea would somehow undermine her resolve to go through with it if it should turn out to be economically viable. Moreover, she knew that it would not be easy offering her home to strangers. Her emotions might show and she did not wish Justin to see them. But now she wished he were here. The man and woman seated opposite her unnerved her. The woman was very smart in an expensive way, with hard calculating eyes. She had not troubled to conceal her disapproval of Harriet's torn jeans and faded shirt. Harriet had no doubt that those same piercing blue eyes would note every faded cushion and carpet, every piece of peeling plaster, every scrap of dust she and old Margaret had left lying on the polished furniture as they had scrambled round the house in hurried preparation for their visitors.

'She'll never live here,' Harriet told herself. 'So don't get in a flap about the fantastic money he's offering. It won't happen. It can't.'

Yet something in the quiet firm tones of the man impressed her with their determination. He, too, looked smartly dressed in a checked country suit with a rather attractive tangerine coloured shirt and tie in a deeper shade. He was not so much handsome as rugged. His accent was unfamiliar, unlike the woman's broad nasal tones, yet sounding Atlantic in origin.

'Are you an American?' she asked impulsively and blushed at the awareness of her gaucherie. It was none of her business and it was more than likely he'd tell her so.

To her surprise, the face, until now granite hard and expressionless, broke into an amused smile. Instantly, it became very attractive.

'No, I'm not, Miss Rothman. I'm from Birmingham. Some people think I'm a Canadian, but in fact I'm Midlands. I hope my simple origins won't prejudice you against me as your tenant?'

Harriet knew he was teasing her and yet she could not bring herself to reply in the same bantering tone; she was too embarrassed.

'Of course not!' she said, cross with herself and with him. 'Now, please, don't you think you and your wife should see the rest of the house and the garden before we talk any more?'

The little boy who had been crouching on the cushioned window seat staring out into the garden made no move as the two adults rose to their feet. The man went across to him and gently laid a hand on the child's shoulder.

'Do you want to come with us, Peter?'

The boy did not turn his head or move. Harriet had realised as soon as they entered the house that something was wrong with the child. He did not look mentally abnormal—in fact he was exceptionally attractive, with huge dark eyes and a delicate heart-shaped face, but it seemed to her almost at once that he must be a deaf-mute, for he appeared neither to hear nor speak and paid no attention to either adult accompanying him.

She was surprised, therefore, to hear Mr Blake talking to him.

'Pete, do you want to come with us?' he said again.

'Lift him down, Martin!' The woman's voice was sharp, edged with irritation. 'You know it's useless asking him. *Make* him come.'

The man hesitated, staring out of the window as if following the boy's gaze.

'There's a squirrel on the lawn!' he said. 'I think Pete is watching it. Maybe we should

30

leave him here.'

Without quite knowing why, Harriet said impulsively:

'If you like I'll stay here and look after him while you wander round. You'd probably rather see the place alone anyway.'

Martin Blake swung round, staring at her.

'Thank you!' he said after a brief pause. 'He seems so interested, absorbed. I . . . I don't want to disturb him. Perhaps I should explain my son is autistic. That is to say . . .' for the first time, the firm measured voice became halting, uncertain, filled with a pain that Harriet could only sense. She said quickly:

'Yes, I know about autistic children. I'm studying psychology at university and we were reading about this problem last term. Don't worry about him. I'll see he doesn't come to any harm.'

The man nodded and taking the woman's arm, went quickly out of the room. As they left Harriet heard the woman say:

'Don't you think that's plain risky, Martin? If Peter throws one of his fits . . .'

Martin Blake's voice, sharp and cutting, broke in with: 'Hush, Molly. He'll be all right. I'm telling you.'

Harriet went over to the window seat and sat down beside the child. How old would he be, she wondered? Three, four, five? He was beautiful, slightly Italianate with his delicate pale face and enormous brown, thickly lashed eyes. Like his father's! The hair was similar, too, thick and curly. Only the mouth was different. The child's was soft and dreamy, ultra-sensitive.

'That little squirrel is trying to find the nuts he stored away last year,' she said, as much to herself as to him. She knew perfectly well that autistic children could not communicate yet she had the impression that he might be listening . . . if not to her, then to the different bird calls in the garden or perhaps to the sound of the wind in the copper beech.

'Last winter that squirrel came to the kitchen window for crusts of bread,' she went on. 'My father called him Squeaker because he used to make such strange little squeaking noises when he wanted us to know he was there. Of course, he should have been tucked up in a hollow tree trunk fast asleep. Squirrels nearly always hibernate in the winter like tortoises. Once I had a tortoise as a pet but it woke up in the middle of winter and died. I was dreadfully upset but my father bought me a budgie instead and I taught it to speak. It used to say "Pretty Polly" which was silly for a budgie! But it learned to say Harry, too. That's my name. Your name is Peter, isn't it? Look, Peter, there's my beloved old pony, Knackers. Would you believe it, he's thirty years old. I can't ride him now but you could. Would you like to come down to the paddock and sit on his back?'

The child's face remained impassive but when Harriet stood up, he, too, climbed down from the window seat and when Harriet took his hand, though it remained inert and ungrasping beneath her fingers, he did not withdraw it.

Harriet walked him slowly out through the French windows onto the lawn. The sun was warm and shone brightly on the boy's dark hair which now had coppery tints.

The tulips were in full bloom in the flower beds edging the drive. The branches of the copper beech were swaying gently, their branches making shadow patterns on the grass.

'I had a tree house up there!' Harriet said and suddenly, tears stung her eyes and she closed them quickly before they could fall. How could she bear to leave this place for three whole years? What would she do with herself during the university vacations without a home to come to? Get work, probably. Even if Mr Blake's incredible offer went through, she would still need money.

They neared the paddock, and Knackers whinnied and came ambling over to them.

'What about *you*?' she said to the old pony. 'Maybe I can make it a condition of the letting that they keep poor Knackers. And Margaret and Joe,' she thought, remembering the old gardener and his wife who looked after her father long before she was born.

She brushed her eyes with the back of her

33

hand and looked down at the child standing impassively beside her.

'Would you like a ride?' she asked. 'Knackers won't mind a tiddler like you on his back. I'll lift you up.'

Though showing no sign of understanding, the boy raised no objection when she lifted him onto the old pony's broad back. She held him with one arm while she gave Knackers' rump a push.

'Go on, walk, you lazy old thing!' she said. 'You can walk quickly enough if you think I've got a sugar lump for you!'

The pony ambled stiffly round the paddock. The boy crouched much as he had on the window seat, making no effort to grip the pony's mane as another child might. But his legs were swinging with the motion of the animal's movements.

'I think you're enjoying it!' Harriet said. 'Come on, we'll go round again, shall we?'

'Get that child down at once Miss Rothman!'

So absorbed had she been, Harriet was not aware of the couple's approach. The woman's voice startled and angered her.

'You might have made Knackers bolt, shouting like that!' she said, her cheeks flushing. She lifted the boy down from his perch. 'Peter was perfectly all right. In fact, I think he was enjoying it and Knackers is as safe as houses.'

'Molly!' The man spoke for the first time.

34

His voice was filled with urgency. 'Look, Molly,' he said in the same quiet but penetrating tone.

He was staring at the boy's hand, holding loosely to Harriet's. There were two brilliant spots of colour on his cheeks.

'Of course he's holding on to her. He was dead scared. She ought never to have . . .'

Martin Blake ignored her. To Harriet he said:

'Miss Rothman, that's the first time Peter has shown even the slightest sign of acknowledging another human being. We none of us exist for him. Don't you see what that means? You've managed somehow to make contact. I'm immeasurably grateful!'

Harriet looked from the woman's tight-lipped, angry face to that of the man and from the father to the child. The boy had let go her hand and wandered off in the direction of the beech tree. He was mumbling or humming unintelligibly to himself.

'I think Peter liked the ride!' she said tentatively.

'And he liked *you!*' the man said, his face hardening into conviction. 'Look Miss Rothman, I want you to stay on here and help my sister-in-law look after the child. I think you might be good for him, and it will take some of the pressure off Molly.'

'Martin, you know I don't begrudge the boy one minute of my time. I'm perfectly capable of . . .'

'That's not the point. Peter liked Miss Rothman. I know it. She'd be good for him.' He turned to Harriet. 'You'll stay, of course!'

It wasn't even a question but a statement of fact. Harriet found her voice. His presumption had effectively silenced her but only momentarily.

'I'm sorry, Mr Blake, but I couldn't possibly. I'm in the middle of my university course. I still have three years to do before I qualify.' Her voice softened. I'd have liked to help but . . .'

The look on his face stopped her. For one terrible moment she imagined that this stolid, rugged man was about to burst into tears. Without being aware of it, she put a hand on his arm and said gently:

'If I were free to do so, I'd love to stay and help with Peter, but I couldn't. I can't!'

He seemed to have got himself under control. He merely nodded and turned back towards the house, leaving the woman to go and collect the boy. Harriet walked in silence beside him. She felt his sadness and helplessness as if they were her own. It must be terrible to love his child so much, want to help him and be powerless, especially with all that force behind him that money and success could bring. He seemed to be regaining his composure. He said thoughtfully:

'My sister-in-law is very good with Peter but

'. . . I don't know, maybe she isn't young enough. You're young—nearer to childhood. Miss Rothman, would *nothing* tempt you to put off your education—if only for a year? I'd pay anything you asked in the way of salary.'

'But it isn't a question of money, Mr Blake!' Harriet tried to explain. 'I need money—desperately, if you really want to know. But I must put my career first. Even when I get my degree I still have two years clinical training to complete before I can qualify. Don't you see?'

He was reminded of Miss Dean's statement that some things can't be bought.

'Besides,' Harriet went on. 'I think you may have been putting far too much stress on a very small incident. Maybe your wife . . . I mean, your sister-in-law, was right and Peter was frightened and that's why he clung to me.'

'You don't really believe that!'

Once again, it was a statement of fact. Harriet said truthfully:

'No, I don't think he was scared. All the same, the fact that he held my hand means nothing at all. It could have been involuntary.'

'But it may have meant something. Don't you see, Miss Rothman, I'm desperate. In two years, that's the first sign. It's never happened with anyone else—not even the specialists and people qualified to deal with such cases. Miss Rothman, I don't think I've ever begged anyone for anything since I was ten years old and begged a neighbour to lend me a pair of shoes so that I could go on a school outing. She refused, telling me no dirty little tyke like me would wear a pair of her kid's shoes. I swore to myself then that I'd never beg again as long as I lived and I never have, until now. For Peter's sake, I'm begging you.'

'Oh, don't please!' Harriet whispered. Somehow it was awful to see such a proud man, stranger though he was, so humble. 'I'm sure you wouldn't want me to say yes if I thought it was a mistake. I don't think your sister-in-law approves of the idea and anyway, I don't know if my university would allow me to take a year off in the middle of the course. I might have to take the whole of my first year again.'

'But you will ask them? You will at least not reject the idea completely?'

She wanted to refuse. Neither the man nor the child was of the least importance to her. To put her whole future in jeopardy for such a tiny incident which could be meaningless, was sheer madness. She *would* refuse . . . if she could only find the courage to wipe the look of hope from this stranger's face.

Before she could speak, there came a sudden ugly screaming from behind them. As they turned, Harriet saw the woman bending over the boy, struggling with him as he kicked and bit like a little animal.

'Oh, Peter!' the man said softly, but without any anger. 'Why did you have to throw one of

38

your tantrums now. Now, of all times!'

'Please!' Harriet said, 'don't feel like that. I wouldn't let this influence me. Don't you understand? I know about autistic children. They live in their own world, not ours. Perhaps Peter just doesn't want to go back into the house and leave the garden and the sunshine and this is his way of objecting.'

'You're understanding. I don't know why but I feel you understand . . . a lot of things. Miss Rothman, I would have tried to buy you—sounds horrible even to me now, but that's what I would have done. Now, strangely, I can't. So for once in my life, I'm going to ignore the advice I gave you earlier about making deals. I'm going to tell you that I know your financial position pretty well. I know you are badly in need of money. I could pay all your debts without even noticing it. That's the way I would have bribed you to do as I wanted. But I know that wouldn't be right. Nor fair to you. I understand you have your future to think of and that consideration either for Peter or me should not enter into your decision. It would not have influenced me at your age and I don't think it should influence you. Please forget that I asked you and as far as the house is concerned, the deal is still on. I'll take care of the place for you and you must feel free to come and see it whenever you wish. I never thought I'd grow to give a damn about bricks and mortar except as a status symbol or an investment, but I can see why you love this house. I'll just have to love it for you when you're gone.'

There was a lump in Harriet's throat which prevented words. In any event, there was little she could say. The boy had quietened and they were ready to go.

As the woman approached with the boy, Harriet held out her hand.

'I hope you will be happy here,' she said. 'I have been, all my life. I think it is a happy place and Peter will like it.'

As she spoke the boy's name, his thick eyelashes, still gluey with recent tears, flickered on his cheeks. Harriet noticed and so did Martin Blake. But neither spoke. He took her hand and shook it.

'I'll be in touch through Eastman's,' he said abruptly. 'Come along, Molly. Put the boy in the car.'

Three minutes later the big grey Bentley was disappearing down the drive, leaving Harriet staring after it.

'Well, Hatty!' said a voice behind her. 'What were they like? Ghastly?'

'Oh, Justin!' Harriet turned and flung her arms round him. She was trembling.

'Oh, come on, they can't be as bad as all that. What's more, they looked as if they had the lolly, or didn't they?'

She tried to smile but instead, found herself crying.

'Now, steady on, old girl. You mustn't get upset. It's not as if you'd signed anything. Whatever it is that's upset you, we'll undo it. So cheer up, chicken. You know I can't bear to see you cry!'

Harriet sniffed and followed Justin back into the house, still holding tightly to his hand. She felt quite unnerved and yet, as Justin had said, she had not committed herself to anything but leasing the house and she had no regrets about doing so.

'Let's have all the facts, darling,' Justin said, sitting down beside her on the window seat. 'I'm positively dying of curiosity!'

At first haltingly and then in a spate of words, Harriet gave her account of the strange morning. She only hesitated once and that was when she recounted Martin Blake's confession that he knew all about her financial position. She regretted it immediately as Justin said angrily:

'He sounds a pretty nasty type to me, Harriet. I think you should steer clear of a man like that. His sort can be ruthless and even if the deal sounds fantastically generous, I'll bet there's a big catch somewhere in his favour.'

Harriet frowned.

'I honestly don't think so, Justin. I believe he wants this house for his little boy and money just doesn't matter in a case like that. He more or less said so. He loves that child and I think he was perfectly genuine. But I didn't like *her* . . .'

'His wife?'

'She isn't his wife. She's his sister-in-law. I had the feeling she hated the house and me. Justin, I know it sounds crazy but I'm not at all sure she doesn't hate the boy too. Oh, I know even the father said how devoted she is but . . . I can't explain . . . I just felt she was putting on an act. I wish . . .'

'Harriet, none of this is your business. Even if she beats the child black and blue, it isn't your concern. Forget it. Stop minding other people's business and remember that you've got quite enough to worry about on your own account.'

'But, Justin, if she does dislike that child, don't you see he'll never get well? Autistic children like Peter need endless love and patience and understanding . . .'

She broke off, seeing the stubborn lines of disapproval tightening Justin's mouth.

'It's not *your* worry!' he said fiercely. 'As to Blake's idea *you* should hold up *your* career in order to get a living as nurse to his child—I never heard such cheek in all my life. I wonder he had the nerve to suggest it!'

Harriet stayed silent. She realised listening to Justin's angry condemnations that there was little point in trying to make him understand the desperate need of the father to help his child. Maybe he would have had to hear his voice when he had begged her . . . and even then Justin might not have understood what it cost a proud man like Martin Blake to beg. She recalled his confession about his childhood and the pair of shoes that would have enabled him to go on the school outing. For some reason she could not explain, she had left this out of her account to Justin.

'Oh, well, it's not important,' she said with a feigned indifference. 'Even if I'd wanted to, I don't suppose the university would have let me take a year off.'

Justin shrugged.

'I expect they would if they realised your financial position. Especially as you did so well in exams. However, as you say, it isn't important since you aren't going to ask for time off It was a mad idea, Harry, and I object very strongly to that man playing on your sympathy. You've always been hopelessly weak where kids are concerned. What you need, darling, is a few of your own.'

He turned to put his arms round her and Harriet let herself be enfolded although at the same time, she hid her face against his jersey so that his kiss fell on the top of her head. She did not want to have to think about her relationship with Justin at this moment. One emotional upheaval at a time was quite enough. She felt drained, exhausted although it was not yet lunch-time. She knew if she gave Justin even half a chance, he would try once more to persuade her to marry him.

'You really do need looking after, darling,' he was saying. 'If I turn my back for a few minutes, you get yourself all tangled up—and with complete strangers, too. Are you really going to let them rent the house?'

'Yes, I am!' Harriet said with a firmness which surprised her as much as Justin. 'He'll take care of it, I know. And I think he'll meet my conditions. I want him to keep Margaret and Joe and I want him to look after poor old Knackers, too. He only wants the house for three years and then I'll be able to come back.'

'Darling!' Justin's voice was hesitant. 'In three years time we'll be married and have a house of our own. You won't need Swallow Grange.'

Slowly, Harriet withdrew herself from his embrace. She was frowning.

'But we could live here, Justin. It could be *our* home!'

'Darling, don't be a ninny. I'll be a fully fledged doctor and have a practice some-where. As you well know, I want to go somewhere where I can really get some experience—lots of work and interest. There's next to nothing to do in a village community like this. I'd be bored to tears.'

Harriet bit her lip. This was not new. Justin had often spoken of his ambitions and he was far too active and enthusiastic ever to settle in a backwater, delivering a few babies and coping with an occasional carbuncle or an outcrop of measles. She'd always known how he felt and yet she had never really contemplated leaving Swallow Grange for ever. She'd always imagined her father would still be living there; that the house would be waiting like her father for Justin and her to come visiting at weekends and on holidays.

'It's my home, Justin!' she said childishly.

His face took on an expression of semi-indulgence, semi-pity.

'Darling, you obviously haven't begun to face facts yet. It would have been different if your father had lived. Anyway, Harry, your home will be with me. I'll make up for Swallow Grange, I promise. You won't have time to miss the place. You'll be far too busy keeping house for me and doing your clinical training, remember? You wouldn't be able to live here any more than I could.'

Justin was right, of course. She, too, was ambitious for the future. Her work at the university fascinated her. She had been wildly impatient for the three years to pass so that she could begin her actual clinical training and perhaps put into practice some of her own ideas combined with the knowledge she was greedily assimilating. But for some inexplicable reason—perhaps it was just a late reaction to her father's death—her future career no longer beckoned with the same urgency. Could it be because she had always sought honours to please her father? That his pride in her achievements was the spur to her ambition and now was gone?

Or could it be that she was unable to forget that look of despairing appeal in Martin Blake's eyes or the more pathetic memory of a little boy lost in a world from which she and maybe only she, could save him?

CHAPTER THREE

Martin drove the big Bentley back towards London in total silence. The boy had fallen asleep on the back seat. Molly Bradbury, too, was silent. Her mouth was tightly closed as she tried to get a hold on her emotions. Inside that cool, perfect exterior, she was violently disturbed.

She had given three years of her life so far in an effort to make Martin fall in love with her. They had been three years of near hell; three years' in which she had had to stifle every natural emotion and play a part ill-suited to her nature. Hardest of all had been the need to conceal the fact from Martin that she was obsessively in love with him.

She loved him long before her younger sister, June, had decided to marry him. June had always been prettier, more amusing, more attractive to the opposite sex. When

Martin first started visiting their house, Molly had thanked Fate that June was heavily preoccupied with a young American lawyer and showed little interest in the Englishman. At the very beginning the field had been clear and she kidded herself that Martin dropped by so frequently in order to see her! Since June was so often out on a date, it usually was her, Molly, with whom Martin sat and chatted. But after a few months, she was forced to face the truth; Martin never asked *her* for a date. When she had been invited to lunch or dinner or drinks or tennis the invitation always included June. Martin came to their house only in order to see her sister and eventually, June began to notice Martin. It only needed a minor quarrel for June to stop dating her young lawyer and begin dating Martin.

From then on, Molly had no illusions. It was June the Englishman wanted and, as Molly correctly surmised, ended up getting. She kept her feelings totally concealed. Not even June guessed the truth. The day they were married, Molly started trying to put Martin out of her mind. She threw herself into work on various women's committees, filling her days with work, lunches and dinners, the ballet, concerts, cinemas, in beauty salons and department stores, buying clothes she did not really need; spending money with a wild extravagance which was quite at variance with her conservative nature. June had always been the frivolous, extravagant one; the butterfly chasing the sunshine. Molly, intelligent, clever and far more mature, had been what her parents called 'the steady one'. She changed completely after June's marriage. Even her appearance took on a new character. Until then always rather casual about clothes, she now never appeared until the last meticulous detail was in place.

'You always look so incredibly chic, Molly!' June had sighed enviously as she waddled round uncomfortably large and pregnant with her first child. 'I feel such a frump these days. Not that Martin seems to care. He's thrilled to death about the baby. Do you realise you'll be an aunt, Molly? Doesn't seem possible, does it? Aren't you excited, honey?'

Molly was eaten up with envy. She tried to keep away from her sister's home. She could not stand the atmosphere of perfection—the doting wife, the proud attentive husband, the nursery waiting for the much-wanted child. The acid of envy burned almost as painfully as her unrequited passion for Martin. Such visits, especially when he was home, were agonising efforts at self-control, simulated enthusiasm and sisterly affection. Yet she could not keep away. No matter what vows she made as she left the house, within a week or two her feet would drag her back once more. She was like an alcoholic, unable to keep away from the source of her bitter unhappiness.

After the baby was born she forced herself to take a trip to Europe. Whilst in Italy she had a brief meaningless affair with a handsome young Milanese, but it did nothing whatever to assuage her desire for Martin. Within a week she was flying back to the States, driving up to her sister's house, her heart thundering its excitement whilst her voice said coolly:

'Hullo, June! Hi, Martin! How's things? Europe was a bore so I've come home.'

Then she would wait for the crumbs Martin thoughtlessly dropped into the parched desert of her longing—the tiny electric contact of his fingers when he handed her a Martini; the brush of his arm against hers as they went upstairs to see the baby; the absurd yet intense thrill of laying her cheek against the baby's dark hair, the very replica of his father's.

Deep down inside, Molly knew that this kind of obsession was unhealthy; that if she gave way to it, she could really become mentally disturbed. But she told herself that she was more than well able to keep herself in check. Like the alcoholic, she refused to face the fact that she could not stay away. Because no one saw or guessed how she felt, she believed her masochistic behaviour was harmless. She never counted the terrible cost to her own nervous system whilst this situation continued.

Then June and Martin went to the Bahamas

for a holiday and the accident happened. June died and Martin was free. When he arrived home, shocked, grief-stricken and shaking, Molly had been there in his house to look after him.

She was wise enough not to reveal even for a second her own wild joy at this incredible stroke of good fortune. She pretended as great a grief as Martin at the loss of her young sister and almost succeeded in feeling sad. She could bring herself to remember and recount all June's virtues now she had ceased to own what Molly wanted. She had been jealous of the live possessor—not the ghost. She was shrewd enough to guess that a man of Martin's nature could not live for long with the past. He was too vital, too much alive to live on maudlin memories.

She moved from her apartment into his house, ostensibly to supervise the child's care.

'June would have wanted me to,' she told Martin and he instantly accepted it. Molly ran the house efficiently and when he began once more to entertain as was frequently necessary for him in business, she made an excellent hostess and organised the domestic side of his life easily and without fuss. His relationship with her was equally detached and he was grateful for the help of his sister-in-law, having no wish for the presence of a strange woman in his home. Molly soon became part of the establishment and as the first shock of June's death wore off and he began to take up the threads of his old bachelor existence, he was moderately content . . . until the trouble began with Peter.

Molly was not good with the child. At first she found her proxy motherhood easy enough to cope with. June had an excellent young girl who lived in and did most of the nursery chores under Molly's supervision. The boy, though sensitive and highly strung, was quite manageable. But as he grew from baby to toddler, the young girl seemed unable to keep him quiet.

'Must you let him scream like that, Maureen?' Molly would say coldly from the nursery doorway. 'He's getting quite out of control. What he needs is a damn good slap. You're too soft with him, Maureen.'

'I think he's missing his mother. He . . .'

'Don't be so stupid. As if a child of that age could even understand she's gone for good. I don't suppose he can begin to grasp what's happened. Now be quiet, Peter. If you don't stop that noise, you're going to be very sorry indeed.'

A few weeks later Maureen gave in her notice to Martin.

'I'm sorry, Mr Blake, but I just don't seem able to manage Peter any more. I can't keep him quiet the way *she* says,' she added sniffing. '*She* says . . .'

'I take it you are referring to Miss Bradbury,

51

Maureen. Have you told her you want to leave?'

The girl's face took on a stubborn look.

'It was you engaged me so I made up my mind it 'ud be you should disengage me. *She* thinks I'm weak with Peter, but . . .

'Miss Bradbury is probably perfectly right, Maureen. Peter is quite old enough to know he can't scream the place down every time he doesn't get his own way. He needs discipline.'

'But he's only *two* Mr Blake. That's the age they all start playing up a bit but it doesn't mean anything. I say ignore it and he'll soon stop trying it on, but *she* says . . .'

'Maureen, will you stop calling Miss Bradbury "she". My sister-in-law is in charge of the boy and that's all there is to it. If you aren't willing to carry out her orders, then you'll have to leave though naturally I'll be sorry to lose you. You've been with Peter since he was born and I know you're fond of him.'

The girl burst into tears.

'That's why I've not gone long before now. Miss Bradbury's not the same as Mrs Blake, sir. She was gentle and ever so sweet with Peter.'

Martin hesitated. He knew Maureen was genuinely fond of Peter yet he could not believe Molly would be overriding the girl's judgement as to what was best for the boy unless it was necessary.

'Let me have a word with Miss Bradbury.

We don't want to lose you, Maureen.'

Later, when he questioned Molly, he was disarmed by her apparent liking for Maureen.

'It will be a great shame if she does leave,' Molly agreed with him. 'Peter adores her and she's usually very good with him. But he is growing up, Martin, and it's time he had some discipline. Maureen spoils him dreadfully. Of course I know she only does so *because* she is so devoted but it isn't good for a child to get everything he wants. No wonder he screams the place down when he can't have his way. I'm only thinking of Peter. He's getting very difficult and wilful.'

'But if Maureen goes it would put a great deal more work on you, Molly . . . unless you think you could replace the girl?'

'I'm not thinking of myself, Martin. I'm thinking of Peter. He must be our first consideration. I'll take him over willingly rather than see him deteriorate in this way. I expect I can organise a younger girl than Maureen who won't object to taking orders from me. I think Maureen does secretly object to my interference. You can understand it, Martin. She was devoted to June and I'm not even mistress of the house, am I? I'm merely an interfering sister-in-law.'

'That's nonsense and you know it. You have complete authority and if Maureen won't accept it, then she'd better go. I'll tell her myself.'

53

Maureen left and Molly now had total possession of the child. In some strange way, it was as if she were gaining possession of Martin. She spent the first afternoon of Maureen's absence with the child on her lap, stroking his hair. When he became restless she read to him from a picture book, his soft little body leaning warm and relaxed against hers as she rocked gently to and fro.

But he would not stay still for long. Soon he was struggling to get down among his toys and Molly's relaxed contentment gave way to a sharp irritation. His anxiety to be away from her was like a rejection—the same rejection she had felt when Martin moved away across a room towards June.

She dumped the boy harshly on the floor where he let out a wail as his knees banged against a metal dinky car.

'Stop that noise!' she shouted. 'At once, Peter, or I'll call your father up here to knock some sense into you!'

That first day was to be the pattern for the days to come. The swift unaccountable variations of her mood made the child less and less willing to trust her, and he became less and less willing to sit on her lap or be kissed or cuddled the way she so often wanted. Occasionally, she would succeed in seducing him with a packet of sweets or a new toy but eventually, fear of her quick vicious temper outweighed greed and he kept his distance. He kept away from his father, too. Molly threatened far too often to bring his father up to the nursery to punish him. Though Martin never lifted a hand to him, he nevertheless became fixed in the boy's mind as an inflictor of pain.

Martin noticed the deterioration.

'Frankly, Molly, I don't understand the boy. It isn't just you he's uncooperative with. He's the same with me. He used to be such a loving little fellow. Now he's either screaming or miles away in some imaginary world of his own. Something's wrong, I'm sure of it. I think he should see a doctor. If we go on like this, you're going to be ill. You look absolutely exhausted, Molly.'

To his consternation and embarrassment, she burst into tears. Awkwardly, Martin put a hand on her arm and patted it meaninglessly.

'Now come on, Molly, pull yourself together. You've been so wonderful and patient, please don't give way now. Why, if anything happened to you, how would we manage without you!'

'I think Peter would be glad if I left. I don't think he loves me at all!'

There was such a degree of feeling in her tone that Martin was shaken. Molly was in a greater state of nerves than even he had supposed!

'Of course he does. We'd both be lost without you.'

'Oh, Martin, if I thought that was true, I could keep on trying. It's just . . . well, sometimes it seems as if I'm pouring love out and not getting anything back. If I could believe it would all work out in the end, I wouldn't get so down-hearted, but . . .'

'But nothing, Molly. You're just overtired and depressed. Of course it'll work out right. Peter's just going through a difficult phase. When he grows up a bit, he'll realise how much you've done for him and he'll be as grateful as I am.'

'Are you, Martin? I'd like to believe it.'

This was a new side to Molly he'd never seen before. She had always struck him as being incredibly calm, placid, even emotionless. For the first time he was aware of her as a woman and it struck him how selfish he had been in accepting all she had given him this past year without thought of her life, her happiness, her future.

How old was she? Older than June. Thirty or somewhere near that. She ought to be married, looking after a husband and children of her own. He told her so. The expression on her face as he spoke momentarily shook him. Indescribable anger as if he had suggested something shocking to her. But it was fleeting, quickly superseded by a casual:

'Oh, nonsense, Martin. I'm in no hurry to tie myself down for life. Why should I be? I have a lovely home and you and Peter to look after.

So long as you both need me . . .'

'You know we do,' Martin said genuinely. But he still felt an inexplicable unease. 'As a matter of fact, I've got to fly to England next week on business. I'll be away about ten days. Now how could I go if you weren't here to hold the fort in my absence?'

His undeniable need of her, albeit only as a housekeeper, was the crumb of comfort Molly clung to, telling herself that one day soon, when the memory of June had receded into the background, Martin would wake up to the fact that he needed her, Molly, as a woman, a wife. Meanwhile, the torment of living so close yet never close continued. Her nerves became more shredded and the boy's condition worsened. When Martin returned from England, he insisted the child saw a doctor.

Then started a round of visits to child specialists and psychologists. Several times Martin was told that it would be beneficial for the boy to have a new environment, but although he himself felt this might be a good idea Molly resisted the suggestion that the child be sent away with unrelenting violence.

'What can someone else do that we can't do, Martin? Peter needs love and understanding and patience and who can give him more than you and I do? Besides, I'm sure he's improving. He's much quieter than he used to be, much less demanding.'

'Maybe he should spend more time with

other children of his own age. The Mathews were saying the other day that they never see Peter and he and little Robert used to be such good friends!'

'I've deliberately dropped that association, Martin. Visits to Robert always seemed to get Peter thoroughly over-excited and he'd be ten times worse when I got him home. It was the same when Robert came here. I haven't wanted to worry you with silly little things like that. Heaven knows you've been busy enough with your own work without my bothering you unless it was really necessary. Quite frankly, Peter only really behaves himself when he's alone with me. Otherwise he gets hysterical.'

Martin pushed the germ of uneasiness to the back of his mind. He had no knowledge of young children; no idea what a toddler needed. Molly seemed to understand what she was about and he, himself, was loathe to send so young a child away. She was right in saying that the boy was far quieter than he had been; that he was perfectly content to play by himself for hours on end in some imaginary world of his own. He didn't seem to need the kind of physical contact he associated with small children; the goodnight hug; the piggy backs; ball games in the garden. In fact he was totally self-contained, preferring his own company to Molly's or his. The occasional outbursts of violence Molly seemed to deal with somehow and there was little more he could do other than believe, as she did, that Peter would become more sociable, more normal, as he grew older.

He would have liked to see him go to a nursery school but as Molly pointed out, Peter was very backward with language and with his peculiar ways, might be made fun of by the other children.

'He's only a baby, Martin. Give him another year to catch up.'

But within six months Peter had withdrawn completely from the outside world. Martin had been to California for five weeks on business. When he returned, a white-faced Molly informed him that she thought Peter had had some kind of breakdown; that it was impossible to make any kind of contact with him and that his speech was unintelligible.

Terrified that his son might have gone mad, Martin rushed him to one of the best pediatricians in New York. The prognosis was that Peter was autistic.

'But how? Why?' Martin asked when he was told there was no instant cure or even the guarantee of a cure. The specialist gave him a sympathetic glance.

'No one knows what causes this condition. We believe it's usually the result of some kind of shock to the emotional system. You tell me his mother died suddenly; that could have started the trouble. It's impossible to say. There are several places we can send him where he'll get specialised handling and treatment.'

Martin looked at the child sitting cross-legged on the floor, rocking himself to and fro. His heart ached.

'But Peter doesn't like strangers. He's always been shy and he's never been away from home. Surely my sister-in-law can cope at home? She's absolutely devoted to him. Peter responds to her—or he did. Wouldn't it be an even greater shock to him to go away somewhere strange? Couldn't this be just a temporary set-back?'

'I'm afraid not, Mr Blake . . .'

It was Molly who came up with an alternative.

'Why accept one man's assessment, Martin. There are other opinions to be had from other specialists who may be able to cure Peter quickly and permanently. For Peter's sake, I don't think we should give in on one man's say-so.'

'But it isn't really one man's say-so!' Martin said thoughtfully. 'There were those other doctors we took him to last year, who said he should go away. Maybe if we'd taken their advice then, we wouldn't be in this position now. The specialist said this condition didn't happen overnight; that Peter must have been working up to it for some time and we know that's true.'

'Well, he's your child, Martin, and it's your

decision but *I* certainly wouldn't give up so easily and I'm surprised to hear you even consider it. I love Peter. I'd go to the ends of the world to find someone who could put him right. I'd have thought you'd do as much.'

'You know I'd do any God-damn thing!' Martin said wretchedly. 'It's just that . . . oh, maybe you're right. There is another man who's supposed to be an authority in such cases. It means going to Washington . . .'

So the search began. From Washington to San Francisco to Ottawa and thence to London, England. The diagnosis was always the same.

'Give him one more year with us,' Molly pleaded as Martin's resistance hardened. 'It's not quite so terrible sending him away when he's five. But a four-year-old . . . even you can't really want that, Martin.'

The fact of the matter was Martin did want it. The sight of the little boy distressed him quite unbearably. He was torn in pieces by love and pity which made his heart ache every time he saw that thin lost little face and heard the unintelligible mumblings.

With the intelligent half of his mind, Martin accepted that the doctors could not all be wrong and that Peter should go to a special school if he were ever to get better. But the emotional side weakened him. He couldn't be sure that his desire to send Peter away was because he truly believed it would be best for

61

the boy and not because he wanted him where he could no longer see him and be tortured by the sight. He mistrusted his motives as much as his judgement and so let Molly's urgent appeals sway him. He agreed to keep the boy at home until he was five.

He transferred to London because Molly thought Peter might benefit by a complete change of environment. He sold the house in New York and took the lease of a large, comfortable flat in Cheyne Walk. It seemed to make little difference to Peter but Molly was happier. He could not know the real reason for her happiness—that he had left behind him in the States a vast number of friends, colleagues and acquaintances and at least for a few months, was far more often at home in the evenings and at weekends than he had been when they lived in New York.

But the quiet routine of domestic life, dining, watching television, having one or two people in to drinks with Molly always at his elbow, began to take its toll on Martin's restless spirit. As Molly's hold tightened, he began to crave freedom and stayed later and later at the office. Molly sensed his dwindling dependence on her and with the utmost self-control, forbore from complaining. She knew only too well that she had no security of any kind. Martin could change his mind and send Peter away and with the boy gone, he could manage very well without her. Peter was the only fetter by which she could hold him.

She clung to the waning hope that one day Martin would really see her, not as his sister-in-law or proxy mother to his child, but as a woman. She tried every way she could to make him notice her—changing her hair styles, choosing clothes which were most flattering and most likely to appeal to his masculine instincts. But although invariably kind and at times even affectionate, he never showed the slightest desire for her nor wish to take their relationship on to a more personal plane. Like Peter—in his way—Martin was equally remote and unreachable.

When she discovered he was having an affair with the woman, Cynthia, she began to lose her nerve. She went to her doctor and was put on tranquillizers. Although she told him nothing of her private life, he knew she was unmarried and shrewdly guessed that tension and emotional starvation were the cause of her nerves.

'You should try to get away and make a fresh start,' he suggested. 'A new job, a new environment. Put some distance between you and whatever it is that is getting on your nerves. You're an American, aren't you, Miss Bradbury? Perhaps it would be possible for you to return to the States, or travel round Europe. You need a rest—a change, otherwise you could end up with a complete breakdown!'

She had thought him a very stupid man. As

63

if anything or anyone in the whole world could tempt her away from Martin! He was her life—the only love she had ever had. One day he would realise how much she could give him; appreciate her total devotion, love her as he had once loved June.

She looked at Martin's hands on the steering wheel of the hired car as he drove silently and swiftly down the motorway. They were large, square, strong hands which betrayed his working-class origins. She knew every tiny detail of his background and was excited, as always, by the thought of what might lie beneath the sophisticated gentle-manly exterior he presented to the world. That he could be hard, ruthless, violent, she knew very well, just as she knew from June that he could be a wildly passionate lover, forceful, demanding yet tender and gentle.

She tried not to think about her own feelings if he were to reach out one of those hands and touch her knee. Suddenly she was reminded of the girl whose house they were apparently going to lease and the way Martin's hand had lain for a brief moment on that soft young shoulder. A jealousy so intense ripped through her body that she felt physically sick. It had been bad enough knowing Martin had a mistress somewhere in London, imagining him making love to Cynthia. It was far worse actually to see him in physical contact with a pretty girl. And Miss Rothman was attractive in a young, coltish way. Thank God Martin had not been able to tempt her into staying on as a kind of nurse au-pair to Peter.

Another wave of jealousy hit her at the thought that the girl had somehow managed to get through to the boy—or appeared to do so. If Martin really believed it had happened, it undermined her own position quite frighteningly. He might stop thinking, might come to disbelieve that she, Molly, was the only person fit to look after the boy; who understood him. As if anyone in the world would sacrifice herself the way she did, tying herself morning, noon and night to the handicapped child.

She longed to ask Martin if he really meant to bury her and Peter in this remote backwater of England. But there was something so preoccupied in his silent concentration that she decided to save her questions and ultimately her arguments, until he was more approachable. She knew only too well how stubbornly he could cling to an idea once he had set his heart on it. Only very occasionally would he allow her a choice of action if it differed from his own. She always gave in quickly for fear of arousing his antagonism or making him feel that she was trying to run his life for him. The merest tiny infringement of his freedom had the effect of making him close up at once so that the normal outward calm of their relationship became tense and fraught with danger. It was a tightrope she was well used to walking and she quashed the violent reactions that lay festering in her and waited for Martin to bring up the subject of Swallow Grange.

He did not do so until they were entering the outskirts of London. Then he said abruptly:

'I would like you to move into that house as soon as it can be arranged, Molly. I *know* Peter will improve there. I'll get all the details fixed up tomorrow. All you need see to is the packing.'

When she made no reply, he glanced sideways at her pale, strained face and said gently:

'I hope you won't be lonely up there, Molly. I know it's asking a lot of you to bury yourself in the wilds with a sick child but knowing you, you'll put up with anything for Peter's sake, won't you? You're a wonderful person. God knows where I'd be without you to help me.'

'If that's what you want, of course I'll do it,' Molly said, her heart racing with happiness at the words of praise. 'It *will* be a bit lonely, but you'll be there, too, won't you, Martin?'

'Naturally, whenever I can. I'll have to stay in town most of the week but I'll drive up on Friday nights and stay until Monday mornings. It'll do me good, too. I've been working full out for months on end and it'll be good for me to relax. I love that house. It's got an atmosphere I can't explain but I know it's tranquil, happy. I think we're going to be very happy there—all three of us.'

Molly felt her body relax the way she never could relax nowadays without the aid of tranquillizers. Martin had said 'the three of us' as if they really were a family. Maybe in that house alone with Martin, he would suddenly realise how necessary she was to him. And she would be able to let him see the love she had for him which was daily becoming harder and harder to conceal.

'I'm almost beginning to look forward to it there,' she said softly. 'And I'm sure you're right about Peter liking it. Maybe this is just what he needs, Martin, and he really will get well. I'll do everything—everything I can to make him happy. You know that, don't you, Martin?'

'Of course!' he replied. But his thoughts had slipped back to the slim, boyish figure of the girl and the look of peace on Peter's face as he had ridden round the paddock in the circle of her protecting arm.

CHAPTER FOUR

'You're only whetting her interest, Dad,' Justin said reprovingly as his father launched into even deeper discussion with Harriet on the subject of autistic children. 'Believe it or not, I think Harry was actually tempted to chuck her career to the winds in order to try to reclaim the boy. I wish you'd change the subject!'

The grey-haired doctor waggled a finger at his son.

'You're just jealous because Harriet is giving *me* all the attention for once. You go and help your mother with the washing up and leave us to our little talk.'

'I should be helping!' Harriet said guiltily, but the old man motioned her to remain where she was in the worn leather armchair opposite his own. They had finished the excellent supper cooked and served by Justin's mother and were relaxing in the drawing-room with coffee and in Dr Barry's case, a fat cigar.

Justin's house was second home to Harriet. She had run in and out of it as a child the way Justin had had the freedom of Swallow Grange. Mrs Barry, Aunt Ethel to Harriet, had been the nearest thing to a mother she had ever known. She loved both Justin's parents devotedly and knew that they loved her. It would be one of the nicest parts about marrying Justin—that her future in-laws were so sweet and dear to her.

Justin went out to the kitchen to help his mother and the old doctor resumed his theorising about conditions such as Peter's.

'I've only come across it once before,' he said. 'That was way back in the early thirties.

In those days an autistic child was thought to be a mental case. Now we know a great deal more—that the brain can function normally but the child has opted out, so contact is lost and the patient seems insane.'

'But what makes a child opt out?' Harriet said. 'I know it's supposed to be the result of an emotional shock but then lots of children must get emotional shocks who never become autistic. Why in some cases only? And why are only some of them cured?'

'Because we're groping in the dark trying to find the best treatment, my dear. I'm very interested to hear the father thought you'd got through to the boy. Of course, it may have been wishful thinking. All the same, if it were true, then maybe you are the right person to handle the child. Not that you're free to do so, but it would have been a very interesting experiment.'

'I wish I could see it as clinically as you, Uncle Jack. The little boy touched me in a way I couldn't make Justin understand. He was so . . . so helpless. And the father even more so. I wonder why he hasn't sent him to a special school!'

'Devoted parents don't always make the best parents, Harry. It's a case of being cruel to be kind. Maybe the father just can't bear to think of the child in an institution, especially since he's not got a wife.' .

'Well, he's got a sister-in-law, though what

69

that has got to do with it I can't quite see.'

'Simply that if his wife were alive, his love wouldn't be so concentrated on the boy and he'd be more detached, better able to judge what was best for the child.'

Harriet grimaced.

'Well, if Mr Blake's wife was anything like her sister, he's a lot better off without her!' she said. 'There was something about that woman I didn't like, Uncle Jack. *He* said she was heart and soul devoted to the boy, but there was something in the way she handled him that grated. I can't explain.'

The doctor laughed.

'Sounds like a bit of feminine jealousy to me.'

'Jealousy!' Harriet echoed. 'What an idea!'

'Not so far fetched as you might suppose. The boy's in *her* charge and you think he should be in yours. You've seen him subconsciously as your patient ever since the father put the idea in your head that you could help him. How's that for a bit of clever psychology?'

Harriet leaned over and hugged him.

'You are an old silly!' she laughed affectionately. 'As if I were really involved! I was just interested in your views on autistic children, that's all.'

'Well, I'm interested in what you've decided to do about Swallow Grange. Do you really mean to let it, my dear? Justin said he thought you were quite serious in your decision to do so.'

Harriet nodded.

'Yes, I am! If I do so, I can straighten out my finances in a few years and still have my home. I'd hate to sell, Uncle Jack. Think how you'd feel if you had to leave this place.' The doctor nodded.

'I understood your father's reluctance to sell,' he said gently. 'He loved Swallow Grange the way you do. Maybe one day you and Justin can live there. I'm sorry you won't let me help in the small way I can, Harriet. You're as proud as your father. He wouldn't borrow money from me either. If he could borrow from Charlie Radnor, I don't see why he couldn't borrow from me.'

'Uncle Jack, you know why. Charlie Radnor is the bank—and somehow that's different. You were his best friend.'

'All the same, he'd have wanted me to help you.'

'Only if I couldn't stand on my own feet—and I can, Uncle Jack. I'm going to get all the debts paid and I'll do it by myself, so stop worrying about me.'

'I do worry, and so does Justin. He wants to marry you, Harry. Why don't you?'

'Because I'm not ready to get married yet!' Harriet said. 'I love Justin . . . I always have and always will . . . but I just don't want to marry anyone yet. I've led such a terribly

71

sheltered life. I want to live, grow up a bit, before I settle down.'

The doctor nodded.

'I suppose that makes sense. You've got a good head on your shoulders, Harry, and maybe you know what's best for you. Just remember that whatever you do, this house is home and you're always welcome, no matter what happens.'

Mrs Barry returned with Justin and the remainder of the evening was spent playing Scrabble—a game Dr Barry greatly enjoyed and found relaxing. As he guessed, Harriet was soon involved in the play and the little frowns of tension left her forehead as she laughed happily whenever Justin teased as was his custom.

It wasn't until Justin got up as always to walk Harriet home that the look of uneasiness spread across her face once more.

'Justin, would you think I was being stupid if I said I'd rather walk home alone?'

He stared at her in hurt surprise.

'But why?' he asked, sounding bewildered and unhappy. 'I always go back with you.'

She turned her face away so that she could not see his eyes. How could she possibly explain to him that it wasn't the walk but the prolonged goodnight kissing she wanted to avoid. Since she couldn't explain to herself why she had suddenly come to dread Justin's physical approaches, how could she begin to do so to him?

'Okay—I just thought I'd go by myself and have a good think!'

She gave an ineffectual smile which did not deceive Justin.

'Something's wrong and you aren't telling me,' he said. 'It's almost as if you are trying to put a barrier between us—deliberately!'

'Perhaps I am. I don't know what's wrong, Justin, and that's the truth. You've been so wonderful ever since . . . since Daddy died. Maybe I'm just feeling guilty because I don't feel able to marry you yet. It does seem ungrateful, even to me.'

Justin's face flushed an angry red.

'You don't honestly believe I want you to marry me out of gratitude, Harry? I *thought* you loved me.'

Harriet bit her lip.

'Please don't let's quarrel!' she said. 'I'm making an awful mess of everything, aren't I, and it's been such a happy evening.'

He softened at once and put an arm round her, hugging her to him.

'I'm the one who's behaving badly, behaving like a spoilt child because I can't have what I want. I'm not being very understanding, either. You've had a long day and I expect you're tired. Let me walk you home, darling. I won't stay. You go straight to bed.'

True to his word, he did not try to persuade her to ask him in for a last drink and chat as

73

was usual, but kissed her goodnight at the front door. Harriet found herself unexpectedly clinging to him.

'You're really much too nice to me, Justin,' she whispered. 'I think I don't deserve anyone as kind and sweet as you are.'

Justin grinned happily in the darkness.

'I'm not sure if I like the adjective "sweet",' he teased.

'You know what I mean. I think you ought to push me around more—the way you used to when we were kids.'

Justin sighed.

'That was when we were kids. I can't be tough with you now, darling. You're far too beautiful and far too desirable. In any case, I only want what you want.'

Harriet broke away with a little sigh.

'We've never really been put to the test, have we?' she said thoughtfully. 'I mean, up to now, we've always wanted the same things. Suppose I said I was going to chuck up university for the time being and stay here as Mr Blake's employee?'

Justin's expression stiffened.

'You know how I would feel about that—though thank goodness you don't mean it, otherwise you might really test me. It *would* be crazy, Harry, and you know it. But I'm not going to stay here arguing a fantasy. Off you go to bed and I'll be round first thing tomorrow. Okay, sweetheart?'

But as Harriet closed the door behind him, she did not go straight up to her room. Instead, she went through to the drawing-room. Margaret had not drawn the curtains and moonlight flooded through the French windows onto the window-seat. In her mind's eye, Harriet could see the crouched form of the little boy as he had sat that morning staring out across the lawn. He was a stranger to her and yet the memory of him touched her with a pathos that worried her. She had no reason to care—yet she did.

'A good doctor,' she told herself sharply, 'doesn't become emotionally involved with her patients.'

But the child wasn't her patient!

Could Dr Barry have been right when he accused her earlier of being jealous of the child's aunt because deep down inside, she, Harriet, had felt she could help the boy?

She shook her head, trying to keep her mind clear and factual. If only her beloved father were still alive and she could go and ask his advice! Though in her heart, she knew quite well what he would have said.

'You must do what you think is right, my dear. No one else can decide that for you.'

'I'm going back to university!' Harriet said aloud. 'I know that's what I should do, what I *want* to do.'

She walked out of the room quickly, as if afraid that the atmosphere still could influence her in some uncanny way. Hurriedly, she ran upstairs to her bedroom.

Margaret had been in and turned down the cover. She had also pinned a note to Harriet's pillow.

'A Mr Blake phoned twice and said would you ring back this number no matter how late you get home as it's very urgent.'

Harriet sat down on the bed with a feeling of trepidation. Had Mr Blake had second thoughts about the house? It looked that way, though why he should feel his refusal was that urgent that it couldn't wait until morning . . .

She glanced at her watch. Eleven forty-five. Surely he would not expect her to telephone him at this time?

'No matter how late.' the words stared back at her.

Her feeling of apprehension increasing, Harriet drew a deep breath and lifted the telephone.

CHAPTER FIVE

Martin sat alone in his office, drinking steadily. He had been there since eight o'clock, fighting with himself. All day, he had tried to put the thought of Harriet Rothman out of his mind—or more exactly, the sight of the girl with his son. Busy as he had been with

76

Miss Dean piling him up with papers and documents to read and sign, the girl's image kept impinging on the pages until at five o'clock he had given up trying to work and had called round to see Cynthia.

But he was not, after all, in the mood for Cynthia's bright silly chatter; nor for the casual affectionate dalliance she naturally expected. He had a couple of whiskies and excusing himself, went out by himself for dinner. At the small Italian restaurant where he dined, he saw, or imagined he saw a young girl resembling Harriet Rothman who reminded him of what he was trying so desperately to forget; that the girl was committed to university and would not, quite obviously, have the slightest interest in trying to 're-claim' his son.

Grimly, he told himself he was building absurd castles in the air. He had no evidence whatever on which to base his assumption that Harriet *could* help. There was no reason why Peter shouldn't have enjoyed the pony ride; or objected to holding her hand. It didn't *prove* anything. Yet there was still another fragment of evidence—that flicker of the boy's eyelashes which only he, and he was sure, Harriet Rothman had noticed.

He left his meal unfinished and took a taxi back to his office, telling himself that he had not the slightest intention of telephoning Harriet for any other reason but to confirm that she had noticed the boy's response. If she did so, it would be something he could tell the doctor; it would mean a tiny ray of hope that Peter was not completely detached even though he might appear so.

He obtained Harriet's number from directory enquiries and put through a call. His disappointment when the woman servant informed him Miss Rothman was out was so acute that he replaced the receiver without leaving any message. Within half an hour, he was on the phone again, half hoping Harriet might have returned but with a message prepared for the servant in case she had not.

He then sat waiting for her return call with an impatience that was so foreign to his normal behaviour, it frightened him. Even when the most crucial of deals had hung in the balance, he had always managed to stay quietly involved in other matters, not so much totally detached if the deal was really important but sufficiently in control of his emotions to know that he could cope with any eventuality for which he was always well prepared.

But this was different. His hands were trembling and he took another drink to steady himself. He could not understand why he felt such a desperate need of the girl's help. It was illogical and he was a man who lived by logic and had used it to get where he was with the additional aid of a quiet, determined, ruthless pursuit of what he wanted. Not even when he had first fallen in love with June had he waited by a telephone with this same degree of nervous tension.

His marriage had been a happy one, his courtship of June easy and straightforward. It had been an ideal partnership. June's background and wealth had advanced his career and she, herself, was exactly the kind of woman he had envisaged as his wife and as a hostess. She was a great asset in every way, pretty, charming, socially adept, easy to get along with, with her carefree, happy nature. He did not expect more from an ex-society girl who looked on life as one happy playground. She enjoyed it when he made love to her and if the whole set-up became somewhat mechanical and lacking in the depths he secretly desired, he was wise enough to know that June was an excellent wife in every way and that it would be wrong of him to ask for a passion and fire of which she was incapable. He loved her very much—but he was never 'in love' and therefore tormented by the impatient longing of an unrequited desire.

After his fifth whisky, Martin stopped pretending to himself that he was waiting for Harriet's phone call just to talk to her about Peter's apparent responsiveness to her. He wanted far more than that. He wanted Harriet to live in that house and have the care of his child. Gone were the higher, selfless gestures of the morning when he had told her to put

79

her career before anything else. He wasn't interested in her career. He wanted to talk her into looking after Peter and he meant to do it—somehow. He'd said he couldn't bring himself to bribe her but he knew in that hour of self-judgement that he wouldn't hesitate to do so now if he thought it would get him what he wanted.

But shrewdly, he guessed she was not, as Miss Dean would have it, to be bought. He had glimpsed that softening of hers towards the child; towards *him* when he had begged her to help him. She was not hardened yet. An appeal might succeed if he could only voice it convincingly. He had to convince her, not for his sake but for Peter's. He simply couldn't go on any longer watching the child lead what amounted to a living death. She'd have to help. *She'd have to.*

At eleven o'clock he began to doubt she would phone him back. He started to wonder whether the servant had given her the message, or the correct message. He'd expressly said *'no matter how late'*.

Quite suddenly his behaviour struck him as ridiculous. At this time of night, no matter what was said between himself and the girl he couldn't take any action on it. There was no single aspect of this that could not wait until morning. Why, then, did he not go home to bed and tackle the problem calmly and coldly next day?

But he remained restlessly pacing the room, every now and again glancing at the white telephone on his empty, immaculate desk, in a way symbolic of his orderly successful, well-organised but sterile life.

When the phone rang, Martin was so startled that for a moment, he stood staring at it, perfectly still. Then he dived towards it and lifted the receiver.

'Mr Blake? It's Harriet Rothman here. It's so late I wasn't sure whether to ring or not but you said . . .'

He broke in:

'No, it's fine. I'm so glad you did, Miss Rothman. I have to talk to you. I . . .'

Suddenly, all the things he had planned to say went out of his mind, leaving him speechless. He'd never doubted that given the chance to talk to her tonight, he'd manage somehow to convince her that her career was of secondary importance to *his* needs. Now, with the wire humming softly between them and with Harriet waiting to hear what he had to say, he felt totally incapable of expressing himself. He fumbled to light a cigarette, dropping his case and swearing.

'I'm sorry. I can't hear you very well. What did you say?'

Harriet's voice somehow calmed him. 'Actually, I dropped my cigarettes and was letting fly a few oaths!'

He heard her laugh. She sounded nervous.

'Look, Miss Rothman, I don't know how to put this, I'm not usually at a loss for words but in this instance, I just don't know how to begin.'

'Is it about the house?' Harriet asked. 'If you're trying to tell me you've changed your mind about coming to live here, I shall quite understand. You . . .'

'No, for Heaven's sake, it's not that. Of course I want the house. But I want you, too. Damn it, that's not the way I meant to say it. I'm making one hell of a mess of this. I'm sorry. Look, Miss Rothman, whatever you do, don't ring off. I beg you. I may sound drunk or mad but I'm not and I *have* to talk to you. Are you there?'

The man's obvious nervousness calmed her own. Harriet said:

'I'm still here and I won't ring off. It's Peter, isn't it?'

His gratitude for her intuitive under-standing was so intense that he felt an actual physical release of tension. He slumped into his chair and in a quiet, desperate voice, said:

'Yes, it's Peter. Ever since I saw the way you were with him this morning, I've not been able to think of anything else. I kept telling myself I only *imagined* there was some kind of communication between you two. I know all about wishful thinking and how it can twist the truth. But I'm not given to fanciful imaginations, Miss Rothman, and I can't

82

explain my certainty rationally, so I'm appealing to you. Please be totally honest with me. No matter whether you decide to help me or not, tell me the truth. You think you could get through to him, don't you?'

There was a brief pause before Harriet replied quietly:

'I can't be sure either, Mr Blake, but I did feel—I don't know—a link of some kind. I know how you must feel and I'm not sure I ought to raise any hope at all, especially as I just can't help you with Peter. But you asked me to be truthful and that is the truth.'

Martin's fingers gripped even more tightly round the telephone receiver.

'You have to help me!' It was more a cry of despair than an order. 'Don't you see, Miss Rothman, you're my last hope? My only hope. I need your help quite desperately. You have to help my son. Will you at least consider it? Please?'

He was begging, he who had sworn he never would again. They were both aware of it and Harriet the more so of the two.

'I have been thinking about it . . . all day,' she said honestly. 'I couldn't get Peter out of my mind but I'm sure we're both making far too much of something so intangible anyone else would laugh at it. Nothing happened, Mr Blake, nothing we could say was real.'

'But your intuition, like mine, like Peter's . . .'

'Yes, but intuition can be dangerous,' Harriet broke in. 'You, quite naturally, want it to be true. And I, quite naturally, was interested in Peter as a kind of patient and wanted to think I knew the right way to handle him. It's wishful thinking, no more.'

'I told myself the same thing, But what about Peter himself? What about *his* reactions?'

'Were they really so different from usual?' Harriet asked gently. 'Or were you just imagining them?'

'No, I wasn't. And you saw him respond, not once but twice. Admit it!'

It seemed an eternity to Martin before he heard Harriet's voice.

'I thought I did. I couldn't be sure.'

Martin let out his breath. His voice took on a new authority as he began once more to plead with her to help him.

'Even six months of your time could mean the difference between life and death for Peter. That's all he lives now—a living death. And I can't bear to see it. I love him. Do you understand? He's my only child, my son and I love him. It tears me in pieces watching him. If you could only know what a fascinating, intelligent little chap he was before this happened. I know I've no right to involve you in my affairs but I am absolutely convinced there is hope for Peter if you'll look after him. Won't you do it?'

'But I'm not qualified!'

Harriet's words were more in the nature of an appeal.

'Nor is my sister-in-law who's looked after him for the past few years.'

'Yes, but . . . but even if I were to say I'd try, it could all be for nothing and then . . .'

'Then you'd feel you'd wasted a year of your life? Is that what you were going to say?' Martin broke in harshly.

'No, it wasn't!' Harriet said, too indignant to be polite. 'I wasn't thinking of myself. I was thinking of your disappointment and my own sense of failure.'

'I'm sorry, Miss Rothman. Please forgive me and please try to understand. My life has been confined more or less exclusively to business and I'm cynical enough these days to suspect everyone of being totally self-absorbed. I'm not used to dealing with philanthropists. To tell you the truth, I'm not too hot on psychology unless it's in business matters. The only truly unselfish person I know is Molly, my sister-in-law. I always look on her as the one exception in a world of self-seekers. Do you understand?'

'I'm not sure!' Harriet answered truthfully. It seemed such an extraordinary conversation to be having with a strange man at this time of night. 'All I do know is that we've been talking for nearly twenty minutes and it's terribly late. Couldn't we continue in the morning?'

To her surprise, he laughed, sounding almost happy.

'Yes, we can and I apologise again for keeping you up. Will you meet me for lunch? Here in London? Or if that's difficult, I'll drive up to Swallow Grange.'

'But you've only just driven all this way and back!' Harriet said astonished.

'What's that got to do with it? I'll meet you at that strange little pub in the village—what's it called, The Fox? I'll meet you there at twelve-thirty.'

It was on the tip of Harriet's tongue to refuse but he gave her no chance.

'I won't be counting on miracles,' he said before she could speak. 'I know you may very well go on refusing to help Peter but I am counting on finding some way to persuade you. I can't do it on the telephone. Anyway, I've had too much whisky. I'll be more coherent tomorrow. Twelve-thirty. Okay? You'll be there?'

'All right, I'll be there!' Harriet said weakly.

The telephone went dead. Immediately it did so, she regretted her words. It was not only silly but unkind to prolong his hopes. She would not let him persuade her. And if her answer was to be 'no', then it would have been far better to have told him at once. Now he would be certain to think she was weakening.

'And I'm not!' Harriet said to herself firmly. 'I'm going back to university and nothing and no one is going to dissuade me.'

As she climbed into bed both mentally and physically exhausted from the long emotional day, she resolved to telephone first thing in the morning and cancel the lunch date. Neither the child, Peter, nor his father, Martin Blake, were anything to do with her. She would forget them both and the whole crazy idea that she might help the boy.

It was only as she was on the point of falling asleep that she remembered she had already refused twice and her 'no' had not been taken as final. Tomorrow she would make sure that Martin Blake knew she meant what she said.

CHAPTER SIX

At twelve-fifteen, Harriet climbed into the old Morris Traveller and drove into the village. She had changed from jeans into a smart pair of yellow trousers with a white blouse and a sleeveless brown suede jerkin. She had no wish to make the impeccably turned out Mr Blake feel embarrassed by lunching with a tramp, even if it was only in The Fox. And apart from embarrassing him, the thought that she looked her best would give her the confidence she felt more and more in need of every moment that went by.

Margaret had allowed her to sleep late.

When she had brought in Harriet's breakfast at ten o'clock, she had stayed to gossip. Inevitably Harriet had confided in her her plans for renting the house and finally, Mr Blake's plans for her to remain in it!

Margaret had nodded as if it were all perfectly natural. The old servant's comments had undermined Harriet's decision of the previous evening.

'I don't see what harm there is in lunching with the gentleman and talking it over,' Margaret had said. 'After all, Miss Harriet, there's God's purpose in everything that happens to us and maybe it's intended for you to help the poor little boy. Maybe his father is quite right and it *is* only you as can help him.'

'But my career . . .' Harriet pleaded. 'You know what store Daddy set by it and I can't just throw it over for total strangers.'

'Well, Miss Harriet, there's more ways of learning than book learning, I say, and you're that young, you've plenty of time for your career after you've tried to help others as need it.'

'Maggie, you aren't trying to tell me you agree with Mr Blake? You don't really think I should stay?'

'It's not for me to say, or decide for you. You have to do what you think is right, Miss Harriet. All I do say is, why ask me what I think if you're sure in your own mind? And if you're not sure, then maybe you should go to

88

lunch with the gentleman and listen to what he's got to say.'

'That will only confuse me more!' Harriet retorted, not without a shade of bitterness.

Nevertheless, she was driving into the village and hoping against hope that Martin Blake would not keep their date. But as she had known all along, he was there waiting. As she parked her car in the minute space outside the pub, she recognised the big grey Bentley from yesterday.

He was sitting in the bar talking easily and fluently to the publican, Mr Cooper.

Unseen, Harriet was able to pause for a moment and regain her equilibrium. He was so much taller, broader, than she had remembered. And darker. She had forgotten how black his hair was, with not a hint of grey in it. He was a man whose age was impossible to judge. He might be anything from twenty-five to thirty-five, although his manner indicated the latter as more befitting someone of his self assurance and his position in life. He looked strong, powerful, successful—in fact anything but a man with a great overriding tragedy in his life. Two tragedies, in fact, since he was a widower.

At that moment he turned, and recognising her, came forward quickly to welcome her. After last night's extraordinary conversation on the telephone, the meeting might have been constrained and awkward but somehow he contrived to make it casual, easy. During lunch he talked freely about his life in America, avoiding anything personal and frequently making Harriet laugh—something she had certainly not expected to do at this meeting.

Over coffee in the small deserted lounge, Harriet herself reminded him of the object of their rendezvous.

'You've come a very long way to talk about Peter,' she said. 'Don't you think we ought to get things straightened out before you have to go home?'

His face and eyes suddenly serious, he nodded his head and looking directly at her, said:

'I suppose I have been behaving rather like the proverbial ostrich. So long as I avoided the million dollar question, you couldn't say "no".'

Harriet felt herself weaken. There could be no doubting how much her answer mattered to him and she hated the thought of having to hurt him by her refusal. Because she felt weak, she spoke more strongly than she had intended.

'You must know already what my answer is,' she said. 'I cannot disregard my career, Mr Blake, I mean Martin.'

He had insisted on the use of Christian names from the start of lunch, but although she found his use of her name quite natural, it still seemed wrong to be calling a comparative stranger Martin.

'You're very young, Harriet. Is a year so vital to you?'

'I'm nineteen,' Harriet argued. 'I'll be twenty-two before I qualify and get my degree and then I have two years clinical training— that makes four years before I can start work.'

'And it would make so much difference to you if you were to begin at twenty-four instead?'

Harriet lifted her shoulders in an unconscious gesture of annoyance.

'You make it all sound so easy!' she said. 'As if I had years and years ahead of me and was too selfish to spare one of them. But I don't really have so much time. In a few years I'll be married and I'll want children before I'm too old and then I won't be able to work whilst they're small and need me. It would be different if I were a man.'

'You're going to get married?' He looked astonished, as if the idea had not occurred to him.

'Well, I hope so, one day. Justin wants to get married now but I don't think I'm ready to settle down yet. Anyway, he isn't yet qualified and we always said we'd wait until he was.'

'So there's a fiancé. I didn't realise.'

'I'm not exactly engaged,' Harriet corrected him. 'Justin is the doctor's son. We've known each other all our lives and it's sort of understood between us we'll get married one day. But there's no official engagement.'

'You're in love with him?'

She was unprepared for so personal a question. Her cheeks flushed and she felt angry and confused. It was none of his business.

'I'm sorry, Harriet. That's not my business, is it?' he said as if reading her thoughts. 'Yet in a way I cannot explain, your future does seem my business. God knows I'm not a man given to whimsey or even to imagination, yet ever since yesterday morning I've known in my bones that our lives are linked in some way I can't explain. It's as if there were some Fate controlling events—and I've never been a man who believed in preordination. I always believed one made one's own fate. All through my life I've been conscious of every important decision and having made it, gone through with it. Life hasn't controlled me. I've controlled it. With the exception of Peter. Sometimes I wonder whether in fact I did make a decision about him and it turned out to be the wrong one. You see, when he first started to show signs of withdrawal, the doctors wanted him to go away. I decided to keep him at home where he was loved and wanted. Maybe I was wrong. Maybe I was selfish. I didn't want to lose him. He was all I had after June, my wife, died. As it all worked out, I've lost him anyway, haven't I?'

'Can't you send him to a special school

now?' Harriet asked gently. 'He's still very young. If the doctors think it best . . .'

'They *think*,' Martin broke in roughly. 'But they don't know. None of them know, Harriet. There isn't one would guarantee a cure. They're just experimenting with this illness, if that's the right term for it. I don't want my Peter used as a guinea pig for their experiments. He's my son, my child, a little boy who has the right to be loved and cared for to the best of my ability. How can strangers care the way Molly and I do? She's fanatically devoted to him, you know. I think if it were not for her, I would have let the doctors have a go with him. But Peter's her life and no one could give him the same degree of love and attention she does.'

Harriet stayed silent, remembering the tall, angular woman with those dark brooding eyes and tight, nervous mouth. She had the look of a neurotic, her face humourless and tense.

'Your sister-in-law isn't married?' she asked curiously.

Martin shook his head.

'No! It's a funny thing, as a matter of fact, but she never has taken much interest in the opposite sex. When I first met my wife, Molly was unquestionably the wilder of the two sisters—always rushing about enjoying herself in the rather frivolous empty way rich young women do. But after June died—she suddenly chucked up all her friends and came to keep house for me and care for Peter. It seemed to be what she wanted and naturally I was delighted to have her help. At times I've felt she ought to be living her own life, meeting people, perhaps marrying and having kids of her own. But whenever I've suggested it—and she's not all that young any more—she looks positively offended and tells me I don't know what I'm talking about—that Peter and I are all the "family" she needs and that she's perfectly happy.'

'She's in love with him!' Harriet thought suddenly and felt guilty, as if prying into another woman's personal secrets. It was equally clear that Martin had no idea of it.

'I still feel Molly ought to get out more than she does. That's another reason, though only incidental, why your coming to help with Peter would leave her free. At the moment she's hopelessly tied to him and it can't be good for her. However, that's beside the point. It's Peter I'm thinking about as you know.'

He turned and stared out of the small dusty window on to the village square. Watching him, Harriet was appalled to see that his eyes were clouded with tears. She was shocked and touched and thoroughly unnerved.

'I'd like to be able to help you, you know that,' she said. 'You seem so sure that I can, so convinced. I think it would be a terrible gamble and you know, it might not work out the way you think. For one thing, how would your sister-in-law feel about handing Peter over to me? She might not like it.'

Martin turned and stared at Harriet.

'Molly is sure to want what's best for Peter. She always has.'

'But she may not think I'm best for him!' Harriet pursued the matter. 'On the face of it, what is there to substantiate your faith in me? I'm unqualified, very young, inexperienced. How can you expect her to accept I may be able to reach Peter when you and she have not?'

Martin bit his lip.

'I could not allow Molly's opinions to influence me. In any event, I'm quite sure she will agree to anything I want.'

His arrogance did not escape Harriet though he was obviously oblivious to it himself. For a moment Harriet felt pity for the sister-in-law though she did not like her.

Once again he seemed to divine her innermost thoughts, for he said, smiling:

'I expect you think I'm used to getting my own way and I suppose it's true. But believe me, Harriet, I never take anything for granted, despite what I may say which makes you think otherwise. Least of all do I take you for granted. No one could be more aware than I that I have no claim on your time, even on your sympathy. I can't even appeal to your intelligence because I accept that the intelligent thing for you to do is to ignore my problems and get on with your own life. Nevertheless, I *am* appealing to you because I truly believe you're the only person in the world who can help Peter. Therefore I need you. He needs you. Please, Harriet, help us!'

More to evade having to give her reply than because she really wished to know, Harriet said:

'When did you first find Peter was autistic?'

'How can I answer that!' Martin said despairingly. If you mean when did I first notice there was something wrong with him, I suppose the answer is not long after my wife died. In retrospect, and in view of what the doctors have told me, I suppose it could have begun earlier. He was an exceptionally well behaved, contented baby and provided he had a regular routine, neither my wife nor the girl who was more or less his Nanny, ever had any trouble with him. I'm told this is typical of autistic babies but remembering how he was— so happy always, chuckling and gurgling when I lifted him up and played silly nonsense games the way one does with babies. He was beautiful, too—but then I've been told most autistic children are physically perfect.'

Harriet nodded. This much confirmed the little she had read on the subject.

'If only someone would give me some rigid guide line!' Martin said in a voice harsh with emotion. 'But they were all so vague—maybe this, maybe that, maybe he'll re-cover, maybe if you send him to a special residential nursery. If Peter had been a mental defective, they'd have said "operate or not operate"; he can be cured or he can't. It's this terribly feeling of helplessness and not knowing what to do for the best. Molly seemed to think love was enough but he became worse and worse, or else it was simply that as he got older we noticed it more. I can't say which day I realised he was looking at me but not seeing me and that no matter what I did to try to attract him, he was totally deaf to my voice. But he isn't deaf. I've seen him listen—especially to music. Yesterday he was listening to the birds in your big beech tree. He *can* hear, but he doesn't want to hear us, hear people. He doesn't want *anything*."

'I think he wanted to stay on Knackers, my pony, when I gave him a ride yesterday afternoon. He seemed to like the rhythm.'

Martin's eyes lit up with sudden enthusiasm.

'I know. And it's true, he does like rhythm. At night he rocks himself to sleep in his cot, back and forward until I think I'll go crazy. Sometimes for days on end, that is all he will do, sit in his cot or in the centre of the floor where Molly has put him just rocking. It's not life, it's death, a living death and I can't bear it much longer.'

There was such anguish in his voice that if Harriet had ever had occasion to doubt his love for the child, she never would again.

He leant across the table, so immersed in his thoughts that he did not notice the empty coffee cup he overturned as he said:

'I wouldn't admit this to another living soul but I can tell you because I feel you'll understand—there have been moments when I've wanted to pick Peter up and scream and shout at him, shake him back into reality; to slap him, even bang his head against a wall—anything to bring some spark of recognition into his face that I exist. You don't know what it's like, living with someone to whom you are invisible—just not there. You begin to doubt your own identity!'

He broke off, his emotion giving way to a new look of despair. Then he gave a bitter smile.

'Not the thing to say to you, is it, whilst trying to persuade you to take on a task I'm busy telling you is insupportable!'

Harriet drew a deep breath.

'Perhaps not, but oddly enough your honesty has made me realise just why you feel you need my help so desperately. I think I understand now why you've been so . . . so very persistent. I don't know if I could help. I really don't know. If I were sure . . .'

Martin grabbed her hand in an unconscious movement of possession.

'Don't you see, there isn't any certainty about anything to do with Peter—none at all. That *you* are uncertain . . . what difference does it make? If you fail then Peter is no worse off. If you were to succeed . . .'

'Autistic children *have* been "re-claimed"!' Harriet said slowly. 'It *has* happened and if it has been done, it could be done again if one only knew how. I don't *know* how.'

'Nor do the experts!' Martin broke in swiftly. 'It's all merely using intuition, guess-work, trial and error. If that's what the experts do, why can't you? It's not so long since you were a child yourself. Maybe you'll get closer to him than I can; or Molly. Certainly neither of us ever thought to give the boy a ride on a horse. He seems afraid of most animals. Yet you put him on the pony as a simple matter of course, remembering, no doubt, your own pleasure in riding it. You did naturally what we would never have done. How can I know what a baby—a sick one at that—needs? I'm not his mother. Maybe if she'd been alive . . .'

'It could have happened just the same and at least now she doesn't know.'

Martin's face softened. He looked at Harriet with a new attitude. For the first time, he was seeing her not just as Peter's possible saviour but as a young woman.

'You're very kind!' he said. 'And sensitive, too. I don't think I've ever met anyone quite like you before! You're very young to be so mature. No wonder your medical student wants to marry you as quickly as possible before someone else realises what he's

99

missing.'

Harriet laughed.

'Justin doesn't think that way. Why, he's known me all his life and he knows my faults as well as my virtues. I don't think it would cross his mind to be jealous. Anyway, he's never had cause to be. He's always known I was his girl.'

'And taken it for granted that you'd end up as his wife. And you, Harriet? Is he right in thinking you belong to him?'

Harriet frowned.

'I'm not quite sure what you mean by that. I don't think human beings ought to "belong" to each other in the way of possessing each other; of two people marrying and becoming one. I think each individual should belong to himself and when they fall in love, each gives the other the chance to expand and grow and become more of a person, not less. Does that sound unromantic?'

It was Martin's turn to smile.

'I don't think I know very much about romance. But your opinions strike me as very enlightened and modern. I thought most women believed in total possession.'

'And I think you're being anti-feminist!' Harriet retaliated. She remembered then that Martin Blake had been married and her cheeks flushed with embarrassment. He said simply:

'I'm not, of course, otherwise I'd never have

got married. I think I was luckier than most men I hear about. June, my wife, was very independent. She never "clung" the way some women do or showed any resentment because I was away so much on business. She always had plenty of friends and things to do when I wasn't there. In fact, there were even occasions when I felt my return home interrupted her social life! I was lucky. We were very happy.'

'They say people who have been happily married once frequently marry a second time,' Harriet remarked.

'That's not only unlikely but impossible,' Martin replied without hesitation. 'Even if I were to meet someone I wanted to marry I couldn't possibly expect her to take on a handicapped child.'

For a fragment of a second it was on the tip of Harriet's tongue to suggest impulsively that his sister-in-law, Molly, might be a possible candidate but naturally, she curbed herself from voicing so personal a remark. His private life was no concern of hers.

Martin broke into her thoughts.

'We're digressing!' he said. 'My life doesn't matter, Harriet. Peter's, and yours, do matter. Will you help me?'

The tone of voice was emotionless, the appeal direct. It was at that moment that Harriet's uncertainty resolved itself. If she were to refuse, she thought, then for years she would go on wondering whether, had she stayed to help that one small human being she might have succeeded. Not to try would be to deny the whole purpose she had given to her life—to help others to get well. This was the first time life had challenged her and she was not going to answer that challenge with a selfish concern for her own career. It *could* wait. Peter could not.

'Very well, I'll write to the university and explain the position. Provided they will allow me to return in a year's time, I'll stay and do what I can for Peter.'

He stared at her with a look of such total incredulity, that the tension eased and Harriet smiled.

'Were you so sure I'd refuse?'

His eyes crinkled at the corners and he broke into a laugh of sheer joy.

'I suppose I was. Oh, Harriet, I just can't tell you what this means to me. I'm so very, very grateful. In fact, for once in my life, I'm speechless. I don't know how to thank you adequately.'

Harriet's face sobered.

'Then don't try,' she said quickly. 'I haven't done anything yet and you'll unnerve me if you take it for granted that I *can* do anything for Peter. All I can say is that I'll *try* but we may get nowhere. We have to remember that all the time. I don't want you to hope for anything at all.'

'I understand your feelings. But I can't help

hoping. That doesn't mean I shall hold you responsible if I hope in vain. I don't have to tell you that money doesn't matter . . . I mean, that whatever you need for yourself or Peter, you have only to ask. I can afford it.'

'I don't think there'll be much. I'll need to get some books so I can read up the subject of autism. There is one in particular by Dr. Bettelheim I read at university I'd like to study . . . again.'

'Make out a list of any books you want and I'll have my secretary send them to you from London at once.'

Harriet smiled.

'I can be doing some reading while we wait for you to move in,' she said. 'When do you think that will be, Mr Blake?'

He noticed the use of this surname and corrected her with a grin.

'You said you'd call me Martin, remember? If we're going to be collaborators, then surely we must also be friends?'

It was impossible now that her mind was made up, not to be infected by the man's enormous excitement and enthusiasm. He was like a power house, full of untapped energy that needed to explode into activity. As he finally paid the bill for lunch and rushed off to see Mr Eastman about the house, Harriet realised that it was the first time she had seen him really happy. It made him look years younger and, she thought with surprise as she made her way home, oddly attractive.

CHAPTER SEVEN

There were many more surprises in store for Harriet where Martin Blake was concerned. He was obviously a man who did not believe in wasting time. Before even she could send him a list of the books she wanted, a huge parcel arrived from London containing a dozen books on the subject of autism. Some were actual case histories, others textbooks which she knew of and were on her list. There were also some she had not yet read which she knew would be informative and useful.

Justin arrived as she was unpacking the parcel. He stood staring down at her where she knelt on the floor amidst paper and packing. Seeing the excited look on her face, he said:

'I see The Tycoon doesn't believe in doing things by halves!'

Harriet frowned.

'That was nasty, Justin. In fact, when I come to think of it, you haven't had one nice word to say since I told you I was staying on to try and help Peter.'

Justin's mouth tightened.

'You know very well how I feel about that.'

'And you know I'm not going to change my mind, so why be unpleasant, Justin? No matter how much you disapprove, my mind's made up, so that's that.'

'In other words, you don't give a damn what I think!'

Harriet's face took on a stubborn look.

'If that's the way you want to put it, yes! It's my life, Justin. I'll live it the way I please. I don't tell you what to do with *your* life.'

'Because you don't give a damn about that, either!'

Harriet's face softened and she stood up, straightening her skirt, and reached out a hand to touch Justin's arm.

'Please don't let's quarrel about it any more,' she appealed to him. 'You know I do care what you think of me, what you do. It's so silly for you to be like this.'

Justin drew his arm angrily from her hand.

'I'm not the one who is being silly. It's a crazy decision and in your heart of hearts, you must know it. As to your caring about me— well, I'm beginning to doubt that, Harry. Delaying your degree means delaying our marriage another year, too. Had you thought of that?'

Harriet's arm dropped to her side. She realised now why Justin was behaving so churlishly. Yet how could she reassure him when deep down she knew he was right. The thought of postponing her marriage a further year had not crossed her mind as a fact to be considered. She'd cared about her career and had forgotten her love-life. No wonder he was hurt. But honesty forbade the easy consolation she could give with a few words of reassurance. She could not possibly say: 'But I want to marry you more than anything else in the world' when it was so patently not true. She was putting a handicapped child first and her career next. Marriage to Justin came a poor third on the list.

'Obviously you *hadn't* given it a thought!' Justin's voice was hard and cold. 'Well, I think you owe it to me, Harry, to tell me some home truths. To start with, aren't you in love with me any more?'

Harriet looked at Justin's unresisting back with a feeling of helplessness. She didn't want to discuss love now.

'What do you want me to say, Justin? I don't feel any differently towards you than I did yesterday or last week or last year. I've always loved you. You know that.'

Now Justin turned and looked directly at her. His eyes were penetrating and narrowed.

'And that's about the whole truth, Harriet. You've never really been "in love" with me. I'm just someone who's always been there— the "steady"; the one you could take for granted. You don't begin to know what being "in love" means. Why, you love me the same way you love that wretched old pony of yours, the way you loved your father; the way you love my father, or mother, or old Margaret.

We're all just as important, but not indispensable in your life.'

'That's not true!' Harriet cried. 'You know I couldn't do without any of you. You . . .'

'There you are, Harriet—I quote your own words, "any of you". I belong with all the rest of your loves. Well, it's not good enough. I thought I could sit back patiently and wait for you to grow up and feel the same way about me as I feel about you. I can see that I've been living in a dream-world. Because I wanted it so much, I was sure it would happen. But it isn't going to happen, is it? Not now or ever!'

His words fell about her like icy drops of rain. The terrible part about it was that they sounded so like the truth. Maybe Justin had not been the only one living in a dream-world, believing as he had that one day she would marry him and belong to him . . .

Belong. The word revived that strange conversation two days ago with Martin Blake. She recalled his question clearly, even the intonation of his voice: *'And you, Harriet, do you belong to him?'*

She had replied that she felt it was wrong for two individuals to 'belong' that way. Yet she had used the very word herself in describing the future she had always envisaged—'to marry Justin and belong to him.'

She looked up from the confusion of her thoughts to find Justin staring at her.

'You don't seem to have anything very

reassuring to say on the subject, do you?'

She stared back at him miserably.

'I don't know what to say, Justin. I don't know what I think any more. Perhaps you are right and I don't really know what being "in love" feels like. I do know I love you, that I always have and always will. But equally, it's true that I don't want to marry you yet, or even think about it. Perhaps I do need time to grow up some more. I honestly don't know. I'm only certain that I love you,' Harriet said helplessly.

Justin's voice was harsh as he replied:

'And I am certain you do not. But there's a way to find out and that's to see how much you miss me when I'm not there. I've thought about this several times but with your father dying and you being alone . . . well, it didn't seem the right time to experiment. Besides, I'd stupidly hoped you might turn to me for comfort and let me take care of you. That hasn't happened. You've decided to live your own life your own way, despite the way I feel about it. So go ahead and try it, Harriet, but don't expect me to be around to watch.'

Harriet listened with a mixture of shock, dismay and hurt pride.

'Justin, you can't really mean you're going to walk out of my life? That's crazy. Why, you're the only friend I've got!'

'You aren't going to have time for friends!' Justin said bitterly. 'Have you forgotten what you said to me yesterday? "It'll be a full-time

108

job caring for the child, Justin. I've got to be with him as often as I possibly can—make him notice me; make him realise I exist and that *he* exists . . ." A *full-time* job, you said. Well, that doesn't leave time for me, does it?'

Now pride was uppermost. Flinging up her head, Harriet said coldly:

'You're quite right, Justin, it doesn't. I was being selfish. Stupid, too. I imagined you'd help me, advise me. But why should you? I've taken on the job and it's my affair. I'm sure I shan't need you if I put my mind to it, Justin, so please free to do exactly as you choose.'

Just for a moment, Justin looked disconcerted. He had half-hoped, at the very back of his mind, that Harriet would break down and plead with him not to desert her when she needed him most. But her independence grated unbearably and gave him the strength of will he'd previously lacked, to say:

'Then I'll probably not be around for a while, Harriet. I'm due back in Edinburgh in a couple of weeks' time, as you know, but as I have a lot of reading to do, I may go back earlier. In any event, don't expect to hear from me till next vacation. Perhaps by then you'll have had enough of this crazy set up you've involved yourself in. Then we can talk sense. Goodbye, Harry!'

He did not try to touch her, kiss her. He turned on his heel and walked out through the

French windows. She stood watching as his tall, slim figure passed under the beech tree and disappeared eventually into the lane that was a short cut to his own home.

As she turned and knelt once more among the pile of books strewn over the carpet, her eyes filled with hot, stinging tears. She felt utterly miserable. Forsaken. Justin had always been there. They had never had a serious quarrel in the whole of their lives.

The tears remained unshed as the thought occurred to her that Justin was right—that she *had* taken him completely for granted; just as she had taken her father's love for granted, or even old Margaret's. Selfishly she had assumed a right to Justin's time and heart.

With her usual impulsiveness, Harriet jumped up to run after him to tell him so. But she remained where she was. That she had behaved selfishly in the past was no reason for her to continue to do so. If Justin was right when he said that she didn't love him with the same urgent intensity as he loved her, it was unfair to ask him to continue with a state of affairs which obviously made him unhappy. It might do both of them good to stay apart for a while. She needed time to find out how much she did miss him when he was no longer there at her beck and call.

Slowly but surely, reason had taken over from emotion, as she idly picked up the book lying nearest to her. It was called *The Siege,* by

Clara Glaiborne Park. Harriet's eyes skimmed down the blurb on the flyleaf. This was the story of an autistic child written by the mother who, though untrained and totally inexperienced, managed nevertheless to retrieve that child from utter withdrawal and bring it back into contact with the world.

Absorbed, intrigued, Harriet began to read. When Margaret came in to tell her that her lunch was ready, Harriet was so lost in the story that Margaret had to repeat her question as to where Justin had gone.

Guiltily, Harriet realised that for the two hours since his departure, she had not given Justin one single thought.

Martin Blake was also feeling guilty at his thoughtlessness. Busy as he had been with his arrangements to take possession of Swallow Grange as soon as was humanly possible, he had not yet made time to have the long quiet talk he knew he must have with Molly.

It was quite unlike him to lack courage. Throughout his life, he had made up his mind what he wanted and pursued his decision to its final conclusion without doubt or fear. But now he was instinctively aware that he was dreading this interview with Molly. He tried to rationalise the reasons for his apprehension. For years he had taken Molly's devotion to himself and Peter for granted. He had, therefore, no logical reason for expecting her to raise any objection to Harriet staying at

111

Swallow Grange to work with and for the child. On the contrary, he could expect Molly to receive the idea with the same intense enthusiasm he felt himself. Harriet would relieve her of many of the restrictions and tensions that her sole care of the boy imposed on her.

Yet the warning instinct so strong in him overrode his reasoning. He foresaw suddenly that Molly might resent another woman, albeit a girl, taking over 'her' child. Molly was possessive by nature. She had never hit it off too well with the various domestic helps they had had. Such women never stayed long and he'd known that Molly was partially responsible for their leaving. She resented their intrusion in the house she naturally looked on as her own. No job was ever done quite to her satisfaction. He recalled one woman in particular, a charlady, who had been greatly attached to Peter and cared enough about him to make a suggestion to Molly as to how she should treat the boy. Molly had considered this well meant advice as an unwarranted interference and gave her instant notice, despite the excellence of her work.

In a way, Martin thought, Molly was possessive with him, too, although she never actually interfered with his life or his freedom. At the same time, she watched him almost as if she were guarding him and though he knew it was well meant, he had occasionally resented her insistence on knowing where he was going in case something happened to Peter and she needed to get hold of him in such an emergency. He agreed with her in principle, but nevertheless, having to account for his every movement had frequently irked him.

For the past two days, driving home from work, he had made up his mind to tell Molly of the arrangements he had made. She would continue the role of housekeeper, organising the running of his home and buying what was needed. Harriet Rothman would have complete charge of Peter and his routine. This way, he imagined, the two women would not tread on each other's toes. Each would be required to make a concession to the other— Molly in handing over the child and Harriet in handing over her home. He could see no reason why the arrangement should not be ideal. Yet he had still not said a word to Molly. She had been reserved and uncommunicative since their visit to Swallow Grange and sensitive to her moods, he found himself avoiding the subject he felt instinctively would be controversial.

There was no putting it off any longer, however. They would be moving house in three weeks' time. Mr Eastman and Harriet had been completely co-operative about this side of the arrangement and Harriet, whom he had telephoned to know if she had received the books, had sounded enthusiastic, even eager to begin her task. He could only hope that Molly's reactions would be the same.

Martin was genuinely surprised at the nature of her reactions when he finally plucked up the courage to tell her. All she seemed able to do was to sit there, staring at him across the dining table, from a tense, white face, saying:

'You've arranged all this behind my back?'

He pushed his half-eaten dessert away from him with a mixture of irritation and dismay.

'I'm sorry if I seem to have ignored your feelings in the matter, Molly, but that really isn't true. I have thought about you a great deal. I didn't consult you before I had made up my mind because I did not want you worrying at a stage when there might be nothing whatever to worry about. Harriet Rothman might never . . .'

'Then you *did* consider I might not like the idea?' she interrupted in a tone of controlled violence. 'It *did* cross your mind that I might bitterly resent you taking Peter away from me and letting some idiotic young student decide what is best for him in future?'

'Look, Molly, sit still and calm yourself. No matter what you may be thinking, I *have* been considering you. For years now you've been tied morning, noon and night to the boy. It can't have been easy. I know. I've spent many an hour with him, too. It's not only physically exhausting but it's soul-destroying—that

114

continual rejection one receives; the way he looks through you as if you don't exist. There are times he's had me wondering if I am in fact really there. The strain on you has been pretty heavy, Molly, and I know it. This girl can give you a very well earned break. I wonder if you have any idea how thin you've grown? I could not let you go on sacrificing yourself for Peter when there was an alternative. And young though she is, I believe Harriet will be good for him, help him.'

'Peter's not *her* concern! He's ours, yours and mine!'

Martin nodded.

'But she is going to make him her concern, too. And you know, Molly, she has this advantage—her behaviour will be objective where ours is emotional. It could be a good thing.'

Molly was standing now. Her hands were twisting together as if she were washing them. She gripped them tightly but they continued to tremble.

'I don't see how you *could* arrange all this without at least having the courtesy of informing me,' she said bitterly. 'You can hardly expect me to take a shock like this without emotion!'

'I hoped you'd be pleased—as happy as I am!' Martin said, trying not to show his impatience. He was not used to Molly disagreeing with him. She was usually so ready

115

to fall in with his wishes. It occurred to him suddenly that maybe Molly had lived with them long enough; that she needed a change, a life of her own. He'd no claims on her simply because she was his sister-in-law.

Haltingly, not very tactfully, he tried to suggest this. At once, the paleness of her face became suffused with colour. For one horrified moment, Martin thought she was on the point of tears, but she managed somehow to control herself and in something much nearer to her usual way of speaking, said:

'That's absurd, Martin. Of course I won't walk out just because I'm upset you planned everything behind my back. I'm sure you've done what you believe to be the best for Peter, as well as for me. Anyway, you know very well that Peter comes before anything else. If I could be as sure as you are this is all a real step forward for him, I'd share your feelings. I simply don't understand why you think that girl can help when with all my experience of Peter, and yours too, we haven't been able to make any impression. *Why should she?*' Martin sighed.

'I can't answer that logically, Molly. It's just a feeling I've had ever since we met her—the way she was with the boy; the way he seemed somehow to trust her, to want to be with her, I can't explain it. It's something indefinable in her personality—a calm, and a gentleness, a child-like quality. I really don't know what it is.'

He took Molly's ensuing silence for acquiescence. He knew nothing of the seething turmoil of jealousy that his words evoked. It was the first time in all the years she'd lived with him that she had ever heard him praise another woman, let alone seem impressed by one. Not very long ago she had deliberately dropped Cynthia's name into a conversation. His remark then had been a disparaging 'Oh, her!' indicating quite clearly that she was of no importance in his life. Molly had known she had nothing to fear from Cynthia. But this was different . . . shockingly different. The girl *was* attractive in a very young, untouched way. She had the same innocent look about her that June had had before she was married. Had Martin seen it too? Although Harriet did not resemble June physically, they were a similar type—a type she herself had never been.

And there was more to fear than a pretty face. Harriet Rothman was to work with Peter. Suppose she were to succeed? Martin would be so grateful, he . . .

'Molly, I'd appreciate it very much indeed if you'd cooperate with me the way you've always done,' Martin broke in tactfully. 'I know you can make the whole of this business, the move and so on, easy and happy for everyone. Peter doesn't like change. Remember how unsettled he was when we left New York? It was weeks after that before he'd let you take him out of

117

his cot without screaming and crying. If he somehow senses you don't want to go . . .'

It was Molly's turn to interrupt.

'I never said I minded going!' she broke in. 'But as you yourself have just said, Martin, Peter hates change and yet you are contemplating handing him over to a strange girl when he's only ever been used to me. I think it's crazy.'

For a moment, Martin wondered whether Molly was right. He had nothing on which to base his faith in Harriet. *Suppose he were wrong?*

But commonsense prevailed. No matter how wrong, Peter could not be worse than he was at this very moment. If Harriet failed, the boy would have to go to an institution; if he did not improve, he'd have to go anyway. There was nothing to lose, everything to gain.

Instinctively he said the right thing to Molly.

'Please say you'll help me, Molly. I do need your help.'

At once her face, her manner, her whole body softened. She lent across the table and lightly touched Martin's arm.

'You know you don't have to ask me that,' she said softly. 'I'll do anything you want, Martin.'

There was such forcefulness in her voice that he looked at her startled, a little wary. He was not used to such intensity. Nor was it like Molly to be so . . . so personal. For one awkward moment, he was reminded of a dreadful suspicion he had had, only held briefly, that Molly might be in love with him. It had happened not long after they'd come to England. As was usual with people who did not know them, the strangers they encountered assumed as a matter of course that Molly was Mrs Blake, his wife. It needed only a few minor explanations to correct this assumption but as Molly put it to him one evening, it could on occasions be slightly embarrassing, especially if they were staying overnight at an hotel, he as Mr Blake and she as Miss Bradbury. She had laughingly suggested it might be sensible to change her surname by deed poll and thereby avoid the questions. With no strong feelings either way, Martin had said he'd look into the technicalities of changing one's name and he asked his secretary, the faithful Miss Dean, to do so for him. It proved to be one of the very rare instances when Miss Dean showed surprise at anything he told her to do. He noticed her expression and was amused to see she did actually have a mind of her own. He asked her what was so surprising in changing one's surname.

It had taken him five minutes to extract from her, very reluctantly, that she thought for Molly to change her name would add to rather than decrease the embarrassments. Curiosity aroused, Martin had argued the point.

119

'Oh, I quite agree where hotel bookings are concerned,' said the prim Miss Dean. 'But you don't live in an hotel, Mr Blake, so naturally it's your social life that concerns you more. People who know Miss Bradbury as your sister-in-law will surely wonder why she should have your surname. If you'll forgive my saying so, I think it is quite likely that many will put the wrong interpretation on it.'

Martin had laughed delightedly.

'You mean they'll think we're living in sin, Miss Dean?'

'Yes, I do, Mr Blake.'

'You're not serious, surely? Would *you* think that?'

'I might very well. I'd certainly *wonder.* In fact, since you've asked me to be perfectly blunt, Mr Blake, I wonder why your sister-in-law should want to alter her name at all, when no purpose is served by it.'

Martin had been amused, astonished and finally uneasy. Miss Dean had managed to make him question Molly's motives. His strange, prim, old-fashioned, reserved little secretary had made him think and the only answer he could possibly give himself was that Molly actually wanted people to think she was his wife.

He certainly did not want that, but why should Molly? Unless . . .

The possibility that she was in love with him was one he did not wish to consider seriously

120

even for a moment. It was an unwelcome thought in every possible respect. If it were true, even remotely so, Molly would have to go and then what would happen to Peter?

But such suspicion lasted only a few moments. He rejected it as unfair to Molly, ridiculous on Miss Dean's part, and highly conceited on his own. Molly was June's sister and that was all. There'd never been anything personal between them. On the contrary, Molly was always very reserved. A few days later he told her that he'd thought some more about the idea that she should adopt his surname but had decided against it as impracticable. Molly did not press the matter and never brought it up again. He'd all but forgotten the incident until now when for the second time he wondered if she could possibly be in love with him. As on that other occasion, he rejected the thought almost as soon as it reached him. If it were true, it would be a tragedy. He needed her, relied on her and could not imagine how he would cope with his life without her, not because of his own need of her but because of Peter's.

As he got up from the dinner table, the thought struck him that bringing Harriet into his life might be a very good thing for all of them in more ways than one.

121

CHAPTER EIGHT

During the three weeks whilst Harriet waited for her tenants to move in, she saw nothing of Justin although his mother came round one afternoon to try to 'patch up the quarrel' as she put it. Justin, true to his word, had gone back early to university and Mrs Barry had been concerned because she and her husband had not seen Harriet for so long.

Harriet did her best to explain as tactfully as possible that both she and Justin thought a period of separation would be good for both of them and that nothing really serious was wrong. She had imagined both Dr and Mrs Barry agreed with Justin's violent disapproval of her plans, so she had avoided going to their house lest it should be embarrassing to them.

Mrs Barry informed her that on the contrary, the doctor was extremely interested in Harriet's new job and wanted her to go round whenever she could spare the time to tell him all about it. As for Justin, both parents considered he had been foolish to try to persuade her into marriage before she felt ready for it and there was no ill feeling towards Harriet, only concern for her because she was alone in the big house.

'We didn't want you all by yourself, maybe fretting over Justin,' Mrs Barry said finally.

Harriet felt a pang of guilt. She had been so busy reading the books Martin Blake had sent her and preparing suitable rooms for the family, she had barely thought of Justin. The time had flown past without her being aware of it. She had been so caught up in her study of autism that she had burned the midnight oil every night when she should have been sleeping.

Mrs Barry departed happily enough when Harriet promised to go round to dinner at least once a week.

'I'm certain to be given one night off!' Harriet said. 'My exact duties have not been defined other than that I'm to have complete charge of Peter.'

She did not tell Mrs Barry that Martin had written to her suggesting a salary of sixty pounds a week. On impulse she had rushed off a letter to him saying this was far too much but she had torn it up before posting, realising that the man might feel happier if he felt he was paying her so generously for her time; as if this did not put him under so great an obligation to her. Also, she needed the money. A long afternoon spent with her accountant had finally laid bare all the small details of her financial position. She needed every penny she could earn to pay off all the debts.

Harriet was determined to earn her vast salary. She made a start by fixing up the small bedroom adjoining her own as a night nursery for Peter. Then she and Margaret put a coat of fresh emulsion on the old nursery and stuck up a frieze, so that the room looked pretty and fresh. Not, she knew only too well, that the little boy would see or notice any of it. But she had firmly made up her mind that her attitude throughout the coming months would be optimistic—geared always towards the ultimate success of her work with the child. Perhaps one day he *would* notice the frieze and then the pictures would be waiting for him.

She had a few moments of hesitation before agreeing with Margaret that Martin Blake should have her father's bedroom and the study for his private use. Sentimentally, she had half hoped to keep those rooms sacrosanct but she soon realised this was not possible. It was no longer her house but her employer's and he was entitled to the best rooms. She allotted Miss Bradbury the large spare room which overlooked the front lawn and was bright and sunny.

She needed what little time remained before their arrival to clear away all her personal possessions. Emptying her father's room was hardest of all to do but she packed all the photographs and his favourite books, his guns and mementoes into a trunk and stored it in the attic. Her own possessions she put in her bedroom. The house now looked stark but clean and ready for its new residents.

Their arrival, however, went far from smoothly. The child seemed thoroughly disturbed by the packing that had gone on in London and was crying distractedly when Molly lifted him out of the car. It did not seem to Harriet that this was the moment for her to take him over and after a quick look at Martin's anxious face, she said to the woman:

'I expect you'd like to put Peter to bed, Miss Bradbury. I'll show you the room I've prepared for him.'

But to Harriet's surprise and Martin's obvious embarrassment, Molly said coldly:

'Peter is your responsibility now, Miss Rothman!' and without more ado, pushed Peter into Harriet's arms.

His small body was limp and unresisting. His crying continuous and monotonous.

'Really, Molly, I don't think . . .' Martin was saying, but Harriet broke in with a quiet:

'That's quite all right. I'll look after him. Margaret has some tea ready for you in the drawing-room.'

She carried Peter into the house and up to the little primrose painted room with its frieze of bright blue fire engines. He looked neither at them nor at Harriet, but kept his eyes closed as the tears trickled down from beneath the lids.

'I think you're hiding from me!' Harriet said as if he heard and understood her although she knew he did neither. She talked as she would to any child of his age as she undressed, washed him and put him into the cot that had once been hers and which she had retrieved from the attic. He became quieter and sat where she had placed him, rocking himself to and fro. Within a few minutes he had rocked himself to sleep.

Harriet went downstairs and into the drawing-room. Martin looked up anxiously as she came in and she nodded reassuringly.

'Peter's okay. He's gone to sleep!'

'Well, thank God for that!' Martin said. 'You see, Molly, I told you Harriet would be able to manage him.'

Harriet bit her lip. It was not exactly the most tactful of remarks. As she feared, Miss Bradbury reacted.

'We'll see, won't we?' she said coldly.

Martin gave a nervous laugh.

'Now that sounds positively ominous, Molly. Don't frighten Harriet before she has even begun. Actually, Peter's an incredibly easy child to manage. He never demands anything. He just sits or rocks or sleeps.'

'If you have finished tea, shall I show you which rooms I've prepared for you?' Harriet changed the conversation. Hoping to smooth Molly's ruffled feathers, she smiled at her and said: 'Of course, you may want to change everything round tomorrow, Miss Bradbury, but I imagined you wouldn't feel like making a lot of decisions so soon after your move. I told

126

Margaret to cook a joint of beef and it will be ready at seven-thirty if that's okay. Naturally, you'll give your own orders tomorrow.'

'That's extremely thoughtful of you,' Martin said warmly. 'And very efficient, too.'

Molly did not smile. She did not speak until Harriet took her into the room she was to have. Martin was seeing to the suitcases. Alone with Harriet for the first time, Molly looked straight at her and said:

'You might as well know, Miss Rothman, that I disapprove of this move, this house and most of all letting a young inexperienced girl like you take over a sick child. However, Mr Blake's wishes come first so my opinions are of no account. But I want to make one thing quite clear—I will not share Peter. You will have complete charge and I don't wish to be consulted at all or to have anything to do with him whilst he is under this roof. He's your responsibility and yours alone. And you alone will take the consequences if anything goes wrong.'

Sheer astonishment kept Harriet speechless. How could this woman who by all accounts was so passionately devoted to Peter, abandon him in such a manner? There were so many ways in which her advice and help would be invaluable, his routine, diet. She knew such things were all important to an autistic child—in fact all that *was* important.

'And there's one more thing. Just because

this is your home, don't make the mistake of thinking you are mistress of it now. I am mistress of the house and what I say goes— that applies to the servants, too. I have Mr Blake's authority to take charge and I intend to. And one of the first things I wish you to understand is that I would prefer you did not dine with us *en famille*. Mr Blake is usually tired when he gets back from work and won't want to have to make conversation to a stranger.'

Harriet flushed. In fact, she had already decided that as an employee, it would be better for her to have her meals with Margaret if she were not having them in the nursery with Peter. But to be told so in such a manner hardly augured well for her future relationship with this woman. Since they were to live under the same roof, it would have been so much pleasanter if they could have got along at least on the surface. Harriet herself would never have wished to be friends although she would have made the effort for everyone's sake. She knew now that this would certainly not be so. This woman was her declared enemy!

'I quite understand!' she said pleasantly. 'And please don't worry, Miss Bradbury. I shan't get in your way.'

She excused herself and left the room with considerable misgivings. She met Martin coming up the stairs and noticed how tired and strained he looked. She managed to smile.

'Your room is along here,' she said. 'I hope I did the right thing but I thought you'd be sure to want some drink in the house so I had Mr Cooper send some bottles along for your use, so if you're dying for a whisky and soda, you'll find them in the dining-room sideboard.'

Martin dumped the two heavy suitcases on the floor and looked at Harriet admiringly.

'You rival my secretary, Miss Dean, for efficiency!' he said grinning. 'Are you always so thoughtful?'

Harriet smiled back.

'I've got to earn my keep!' she said. 'After all, you are paying me such a huge salary, it's only right I should prove myself worth it.'

'I think you'd have done the same even if you weren't being paid,' Martin said seriously. Then he added: 'This is a lovely room. I'm going to like it here. I hope it isn't your room?'

'It was my father's,' Harriet told him. 'He liked it because he could look out on his roses. He had a passion for rose trees and he said if he left his window open at night, he could go to sleep smelling them.'

'One day, when there's time, you must tell me about your father,' Martin said as he turned back from the window. 'I never knew mine. He was a coal miner, I believe. He cleared off soon after I was born and left my mother to fend for us. I'll tell you about him, one day. I should think our fathers were about as different as it's humanly possible for two men to be. We'll compare notes!'

'I must go and see if Peter's all right!' Harriet said, excusing herself. But Martin held out a hand detaining her.

'Look, Harriet, I'm not quite sure how to put this but I'm a bit worried about my sister-in-law. She . . . she hasn't taken this move too well. I don't fully understand why but she seems to have got herself into a bit of a state about it. The fact is she's been under a great strain and her nerves are on edge. Please be tolerant if . . . well, if she's a bit offhand, about Peter and one thing and another. I owe her a great deal and I want this change of routine and scene to be beneficial to her, too. If there's trouble . . .'

'There won't be!' Harriet said firmly. 'I quite understand the position. After all, it can't be easy for her handing Peter over to me. In a way, he's like her own child, isn't he? And you . . . well, you have more or less told her by your actions that you have more faith in what I can do for Peter than you have in her capabilities. It's only natural she should resent me.'

'Well, I don't see it that way!' Martin said sighing. 'I should have thought she'd welcome another woman's help. You'll be company for her, too, when I'm in London. At least, I thought it might work out like that but she tells me she doesn't want companionship. I really don't understand her.'

But I do! Harriet thought. She's in love with this man and she sees me as a rival for his time and attention. I'll have to find some way to let her know I'm not interested, nor in the least likely to fall in love with a man of his age!

She looked up and found Martin's eyes focused on her. They were immensely dark, inscrutable eyes and she looked quickly away. He might be a lot older than herself but he was attractive. He reminded her of her teenage pin-up, Omar Sharif, and the memory made her smile. Martin saw it and instantly questioned her.

Harriet found herself blushing and now it was Martin's turn to notice the girl, no longer merely as a means to an end for his son, Peter, but as an extremely attractive young woman.

'If she were a good deal older,' he thought, 'I'd be more than a little interested!' But the thought was fleeting. He knew Harriet had a young man to whom she was more or less engaged; and in any event, he had no wish to complicate his life by starting an emotional relationship which, in view of their respective ages, would be quite inappropriate. He was glad when Harriet excused herself and left the room to go to Peter.

He began to unpack one of his suitcases but abandoned the task when he remembered that this was a job Molly always did for him. She would have plenty of time for such things now Peter was off her hands. He sat down on the edge of the bed and lit a cigarette, smoking and thinking. For some reason, his mind was uneasy.

Was this idea of his, seemingly so perfect in theory, going to work out badly in practice? He'd overridden Molly's doubts and objections and Harriet's, too, without giving the disadvantages any real consideration. He'd been obsessed with the idea of coming to live here with Peter and as was usual with him, had let nothing stand in the way of his desire. But was it going to work out? Was Harriet too young and inexperienced to be able to cope? Would Molly become restive and bored? Would he soon get fed up with the long hours of road travel to and from his work? Would the two women be able to live together in some kind of harmony or was he to be caught between two warring factors?

He sighed. Life was far from easy. There was also the problem of his affair with Cynthia. He had found himself less and less willing for her company of late. In fact, he was beginning to realise that there was little pleasure in taking to bed a woman whose company he didn't enjoy out of it. He'd never had much time for women's society, even his wife's, devoted as he had been to her. Looking back, as he could do now without any sadness, he knew that the emotion he'd felt when he married June was at least three parts desire and only one part genuine liking. June had been pretty, am using, easy-going and not very deep-thinking. In fact, she shied away from any deep discussion or involvement, preferring to laugh her way through life, enjoying the freedom from worry of any kind. She had always been protected from hardship by her parents' wealth and Martin had been able to continue to provide the way of life she enjoyed so much.

June had accepted her sexual commitment to Martin with the same casual good nature. She did not seem to mind one way or the other whether he chose to make love to her or not. As with all other aspects of her life, she was happy to fall in with his wishes provided they did not impinge on her varied and numerous social engagements.

She had accepted her pregnancy in the same way, enjoying the congratulations and added attention of her friends, the buying of a layette and planning the nursery. With the best gynaecologist in attendance at one of the most expensive private nursing homes, June had suffered little at the birth and life had quickly resumed its normal routine for her when she returned home. A capable girl had taken over the baby once the maternity nurse had left and June was as pleasant and affectionate a mother as she was a wife.

There was no ripple on the surface of their contentment.

Remembering the terrible shock of June's

death, so sudden, violent and final, Martin stubbed out his cigarette and walked restlessly over to the window. The tragedy had marked the beginning of a new phase of life for him. At first Molly had eased the repercussions by taking over the domestic side of June's life and continuing the quiet affluent running of his house as if its mistress was still present. Molly had seen that his meals were ready, his shirts laundered, his groceries shopped and paid for, the flowers bought and arranged in their usual vases, the telephone answered and messages taken. There was no hitch in his routine and the first shock of June's absence was considerably lessened because of her. But then the second tragedy had struck, not suddenly like the first, but gradually as he became aware something was wrong with the baby.

Looking back, he could see that he had begun by trying not to see the facts that were all too obvious now. When a visitor to the house commented doubtfully that surely Peter should be beginning to talk, Martin had shrugged it off, quoting Molly, saying that not all toddlers progressed at equal speed and he'd catch up eventually.

When at last he had insisted Molly took Peter to a doctor for a check-up, he'd been shaken to learn that the doctor wanted Peter to go into hospital for a couple of weeks for a complete and detailed investigation. The thought that his son might be mentally abnormal frightened him into immediate action. If there was anything physically wrong with the boy, he wanted to know at once.

But there was nothing wrong. The tests all showed Peter to be physically perfectly normal. Neither was he deaf nor was his eyesight defective.

'We'd like to see him again in six months time,' the specialist said.

Within six months Peter had withdrawn totally from my kind of communication with the world around him. He had retrogressed to total babyhood, making no attempt to feed himself, even to move or reach out his hand to a toy or a moving object.

Now, years later, Martin could see that he should have taken some sort of action when first he knew Peter was not like normal babies of his age. Had there been other children against whose development he could have compared Peter's, he might have been more worried. But Peter was the first and he, a man, had not appreciated the situation. Molly, he thought, could not be blamed either. Peter was not her child and nor was she any more experienced with babies than he, himself. Perhaps if June had lived . . .

But there was no point pursuing 'ifs', Martin told himself grimly. It had happened. Peter was a severe case of autism and now the only question to be resolved was whether someone, somehow, could get through to him, bring him back to the world he was for some inexplicable reason, rejecting. And Martin was counting far more than he knew was reasonable, on Harriet Rothman to work the miracle.

It was madness and he knew it. In business he could never in a thousand years behave so illogically. To employ in a vital key position a young woman about whom he knew nothing, with neither age nor experience to her credit and no qualifications, was little short of insanity. His only excuse for doing so was 'a hunch', a tiny speck of intuition that had no substantiation in fact.

Angry with himself, not a little frightened, Martin reacted to this downswing of optimism with his usual impulsive need for action. He went out of his room and along the passage to the bedroom Harriet told him she had assigned to Peter. Quietly, he opened the door and looked in.

Harriet was kneeling on the carpet by the cot. She was holding up a metronome. Peter was lying quietly beneath the covers, immobile but for his large dark eyes which were following the rhythmic motion of the hand. Martin had no doubt that Peter was not only seeing the movement but hearing the regulated 'tick-tock' and enjoying it. Harriet had not heard Martin's entry and seemed quite absorbed in what she was doing. As Martin watched, she reached out one hand and laid it on Peter's arm, her fingers tapping gently in time with the clock. Martin realised that she was attempting to establish contact of some kind. Gently, he stepped backwards out of the room and closed the door.

Outside, he leant against the wall and closed his eyes, feeling the tension ease out of his body for the first time in weeks. Let Molly say what she wished against this move, he no longer doubted that twinge of intuition. He had only needed to see Harriet with the boy once more to know, deep down inside, that if anyone could help his son, it was this girl. There was something about her . . . some indefinable gentleness, sensitivity, imaginativeness, that he was prepared to back to the limit of his resources. Let Molly doubt! Let Harriet herself, doubt! He no longer did so.

He opened his eyes to see Molly coming down the landing towards him. Filled with this new sense of peace and hope, he smiled at her warmly.

'Ah, there you are, Molly,' he said, going forward to meet her. 'Let's go down and have ourselves a welcome-in drink!'

Her face flushed with pleasure and unnoticed by him, deepened to a dark pink as he put his arm round her shoulders and gave her an absent-minded hug.

CHAPTER NINE

Justin wrote from Edinburgh.

'My darling Hatty,
I must have been mad to walk out on you the way I did last month. I've missed you like hell, darling, and hope you haven't been too busy to miss me just a little bit. If only I could be sure that you love me! But while one part of me believes it, the other does not and that makes me nervy and demanding when I'm with you. I badly wanted reassurance and you couldn't give it to me. Not your fault!

It doesn't excuse my rushing off the way I did. I suppose I was hurt. Anyway, I want you to know that I am still as much in love with you as ever and that if I have to, I'll wait for ever or until you marry someone else.

Mother wrote and told me you don't have any kind of social life and that she and Father are the only people you see once a week for supper, so I've only The Tycoon to be jealous of, haven't I? I hope everything is going well in that respect and you aren't finding it too unbearable having strangers in your home.

A recent letter from Dad informed me that you seemed quite immersed in your work with the child and I think I owe you an apology here, too. I truthfully thought you were being a bit presumptuous taking on an autistic child as if it were no more than looking after a kid with measles. But Dad said you thought you were actually beginning to make some progress which, if it is true, is marvellous and must be very exciting for you.

Hatty darling—no, Harry, you hate the first, don't you!—please write and tell me I'm forgiven and that you do think of me sometimes. Let's put an end to this silence which I find quite intolerable, the more so since it is of my making.

Always your loving
Justin.'

Harriet's reply, written a few days later, was less spontaneous. She chose her words with care.

'Darling Justin,

It was nice of you to apologise though quite unnecessary. You had every right to be hurt and annoyed and I wish I could be as certain as you about that all important little word—love. The fact is, Justin, I don't know whether I am in love with you or not. If to be in love means

139

that nothing else in one's life matters, then I have to admit that I'm not in love. I miss you, of course, and I've hated the silence between us as much as you. I'm very, very glad we're in touch once more and to be truthful, I never believed we'd stop being friends. It just would not be possible after all these years, would it?

However, I have had a lot of time to think about things and I truly believe that it might be better if you could somehow stop thinking about me in terms of marriage. Re-reading that sentence it sounds odd, doesn't it? What I mean is that you should feel free to go out with other girls and stop thinking about me as if we were engaged. I don't think it is right that you should feel tied to me when I am busy claiming my freedom. No matter how much I'd like to be able to do so, I can't give you the reassurance you spoke of in your letter. The truth is I just don't know how I feel and it definitely is not fair to ask you to wait around while I make up my mind. I hope you understand how I feel.

It was nice of you to be so complimentary about my work with Peter. I hardly dare to put it in writing but I think I am beginning to make contact. It is an exhausting, full-time but absorbing undertaking and not without difficulties as Miss Bradbury 'Martin Blake's sister-in-law' can barely conceal her dislike for me—in fact doesn't trouble to do so unless Martin is around. She makes discouraging and sarcastic remarks all the time and I have my suspicions that she tries to discredit me in Martin's eyes whenever I'm not around to defend myself. Fortunately, he seems still to have faith in me and fortified by this and Peter's silent helpless appeal, I continue with hope.

If it would not bore you, I would like to write at greater length and tell you the various methods I've been using and the results, if you can call them that, which I think are being achieved.

How is your work? I imagine exams are pending and naturally wish you the very best of luck with them. I expect your father told you I'm to be allowed back to university next year as this sabbatical will not put my degree in jeopardy.

Thank you again for writing, dear Justin. I sign my letter the same way you signed yours and with equal sincerity.

Always your loving
Harry.'

Although it was a long letter, reading it before she folded and sealed it in its envelope, Harriet realised that she had only touched the fringe of all the happenings of the past month. Her reference to Molly Bradbury concealed a whole wealth of incidents that were distressing and demoralising to say the least.

Harriet tried to excuse the older woman's hostility, certain as she now was that Molly was passionately and obsessively in love with Martin. She had only to see Molly's face when Martin's car came up the drive, or when he telephoned, or when he was in the room to know that Martin was Molly's *raison d'être*. Harriet could even feel pity for her since it was equally obvious that Martin neither saw nor cared how Molly felt about him. It was difficult at times to credit that any man could be so blind, yet perhaps as well he should be since he did not seem to find his sister-in-law in the least attractive as a woman. She remained part of the background for him—a kind of glorified housekeeper who was always there to see to his every need. He took her totally for granted and managed to conceal his occasional bouts of impatience when she was over-solicitous or, as so often happened, over-anxious to break up any discussion between Martin and Harriet that excluded her.

Harriet felt Molly's jealousy like a continual thorn which could not be prised out and festered annoyingly on and off through the day. She tried to keep out of Molly's way which was not too difficult during the week when she could devote herself exclusively to

Peter. In the evenings they had separate meals and Harriet could avoid her. At weekends, however, when Martin was home, he insisted that Harriet should bring Peter down to the drawing-room or into the garden—to wherever he happened to be, and his interest in the books she was reading, in what she was doing, and why, was insatiable. On such occasions Molly was never far off and refused to be excluded from the conversation. She once startled Martin into total silence when she said cuttingly:

'Don't forget, Martin, that we've only got Harriet with us for a year. When she goes I'll be in charge of Peter again so I'd better know what's going on, don't you think?'

Harriet did not doubt for one moment the genuine and selfless love Martin had for his little boy. But she had begun to doubt Molly's so-called devotion, not only in the present but in the past. Molly ignored the child completely during the week and while this suited Harriet very well, it did seem extraordinary behaviour coming from a woman who had virtually been the boy's mother for the major part of his life and who, according to Martin, had selflessly given her life over to his care. Only once had Molly referred to those past years and that was when she had remarked to Harriet with a cold bitterness:

'Peter was once a warm, loving, normal baby who liked nothing better than to sit on my lap and be cuddled. Now I don't exist for him.'

Harriet could understand the woman's feeling of resentment. A normal child clings to the person who provides its needs and gives it love. Peter, lost in his autistic state, had no needs and wanted no love. Unless one fully understood the effects of autism, it was hard to accept this lack of any human response. Harriet could understand that Molly wanted the baby's love very badly—the more so since the love she gave Martin was similarly ignored and frustrated.

But it wasn't always easy to make allowances for Molly's unhappiness. There was the time when she opened the nursery door and stood there, watching Harriet curled up on the floor beside the silent child, a white quilt pulled over their heads. Her lips curling, she had said coldly:

'You can't imagine how ridiculous you look, Harriet, playing tents with a mentally defective child who can't possibly know what a tent is!'

Harriet had tried to explain.

'The quilt is Peter's refuge. If something has upset him, he crawls under it as a way of escape. If I go with him, then he is not alone. I think he senses it.'

'Rubbish. You're wasting your time.'

'It's mine to waste!' Harriet retorted flushing.

'On the contrary, it's Mr Blake's time. You're paid to help Peter, not to behave as

144

ridiculously as he does.'

Molly must have mentioned the incident to Martin because the following weekend he asked Harriet what she was trying to achieve. Harriet had done her best to explain—that she felt it was wrong to allow Peter to remain in his self-imposed isolation no matter how much he might seek it; that in one of the books she had read, the mother of an autistic child had described the efforts she made to reach her child as a kind of siege upon the fortress of his spirit.

Martin had understood at once and asked to borrow the book. Having read it by the next weekend, he asked Harriet if she felt it would be a good idea to follow the book a stage further and for him to emulate the father of the child in the true life story and play with Peter, tickling him and tossing him in the air.

'I used to do that kind of thing before he got ill. I only stopped because Molly thought it over-excited him,' he said.

Harriet forbore to express her own views— that Molly with her strange, neurotic, reserved nature, might have been the very worst kind of person to deal with a potentially autistic child. In any event, the past did not matter. The future did and Martin was co-operative in every possible way. He backed her against Molly's advice and this was enough for Harriet.

There was a growing sense of participation

between Martin Blake and herself. With some surprise Harriet discovered that he was very quickly able to pick up the rudiments of psychology and even to add ideas and opinions of his own. He was intelligent and ready to learn and it was this most of all which impressed her. The man whom Justin jokingly described as The Tycoon was still, despite his worldly success, humble enough to wish to learn, albeit from a nineteen-year-old girl. Arrogant he might be in other ways but not in this and her respect for him was growing.

Margaret, the old servant, was also rapidly becoming one of Martin's admirers although she had no time at all for 'the bossy' Molly.

'Mr Blake may not be a gentleman by birth,' Margaret said snobbishly, 'but he's certainly one by nature, Miss Harriet, which is more than you can say for *her.*'

Molly did not ask for things. She gave orders. Margaret obeyed but only because Harriet had begged her to comply whenever possible for the sake of general peace in the household.

Tactfully, she explained to Margaret that Molly's position was far from easy; that she had to be 'bossy', since she was living in Harriet's house, in order to establish who was in charge right from the start.

Margaret snorted.

'He who pays the piper calls the tune!' she said sourly, 'and it's Mr Blake as pays my wages, not HER!'

'It's also Mr Blake's wish that Miss Bradbury has the running of the house!' Harriet said. 'So be a dear, Margaret, and ignore her even if you don't like her.'

'Can't see what Mr Blake wants with her!' Margaret grumbled. 'Better off without her, I'd say. I wouldn't wonder *she* turned that poor little mite orticist!'

'Autistic!' Harriet corrected. 'And you mustn't say things like that, Margaret. Mr Blake says she has devoted herself to Peter ever since his wife died.'

'Huh!' was Margaret's last word. She grudgingly obeyed Molly's orders but Martin's wishes were instantly and willingly carried out.

'It's them big dark eyes of his!' the old woman told Harriet impishly. 'If I were younger, he'd fair turn me old bones to water when he smiles!'

Harriet had laughed but in a way, she understood Margaret's flattery. When Martin Blake smiled it transformed his whole face. The rugged, brooding heaviness was gone and he looked so much younger that she found herself surprised each time he changed countenance. It was as if there were two different people—the rather grim, serious, care-worn business man and the impulsive, light-hearted young man who could jump the wooden railings into the pony's paddock as if he were Justin's age.

147

She knew now that he played squash several evenings a week in order to keep fit; that he was a moderate drinker and a temperate eater because physical fitness was as important to him as mental alertness.

'I always wanted to live my life, not vegetate it away,' he once told her. It occurred to her that for a man of his mental and physical energy, Peter's apathy must seem all the more terrible.

But at last it looked as if she really were making some progress with Martin's child. Sitting one afternoon with Peter on the lawn in the dappled light and shade of the beech tree, she had idly picked daisy heads and laid them in a row in front of the inert child. Suddenly, she saw his hand reach for a daisy which was slightly out of line and put it back into its correct regimental order. Holding her breath, taking care that he should not sense her excitement, she had put two more daisies in line and the third deliberately out of line. A second time his hand had come forward and corrected it. For several minutes this 'game' had continued but he had then sunk once more into total inactivity and but for the rows of daisy heads still in their neat ranks, she felt she might have imagined the whole episode. Her first instinct was to rush to the telephone to tell Martin but on second thoughts she did not do so. She had no wish to raise his hopes in vain.

But the following day, another brilliantly sunny one when they could be out of doors, she repeated the experiment. Again the boy's hand appeared slowly to correct the lines of daisies. Harriet casually began to form a circle. Three quarters completed, she stopped picking flower heads. The little boy began to whimper. She let him continue for a moment or two and then put two more daisy heads in place. She stopped once more and again the boy began to cry.

Harriet knew from her text books how important shape and pattern were to an autistic child. Deliberately, she left her hand lying idly near the daisies, never looking directly at Peter. The crying continued but, as she had hoped so desperately, she suddenly felt his hand, feather-light on her own. Knowing that he wished her to pick another daisy and complete the circle, she let him guide her hand to the action. The circle complete, she looked up and saw his small face quite radiant with joy. There was no mistaking the pleasure he felt; no doubting that he had come out of his private world long enough to make her hand do what he would not.

When she told Martin he looked confused.

'Why couldn't *he* pick the daisy?' he asked.

'Because if he did it, then he exists and to himself, he dare not exist,' Harriet explained eagerly. 'So he used my hand instead of his own. That is an acknowledgement that I exist even if he does not.'

From the far side of the room Molly said icily:

'That sounds utterly ridiculous and hopelessly far-fetched.'

They had both forgotten she was there. It was Martin who turned and replied:

'But it isn't, Molly. I see what Harriet is getting at. For her to exist for Peter is a vital first step. And after only a month!' He turned back to Harriet, his face alight with enthusiasm. 'I think it's wonderful. I think you're wonderful. Let's open a bottle of champagne and celebrate!'

'A little premature, isn't it?' Molly's carefully modulated voice was nevertheless like cold ice on their enthusiasm. Martin's face fell and Harriet said quickly:

'Miss Bradbury is right. We mustn't set too much store by one small incident. Autistic children sometimes do a thing once or twice and then never do it again. Let's wait a while before we get too hopeful.'

As quickly as possible, she left the room. As was her custom after she had tucked Peter in for the night, she slipped out to the garden for a brief stroll in the cool evening air. That evening Martin joined her down by the paddock where she was feeding Knackers a lump of sugar.

'I knew you'd be here,' he said almost shyly. 'I hope you don't object to my barging in on your privacy, but I do need to talk to you.'

'Of course I don't mind,' Harriet said at once although she hoped very much that Molly was not leaning out of some window watching Martin. If Molly were doing so, she might get some very wrong ideas.

'It's about Peter, of course,' Martin said, leaning his arms on the rail as Harriet was doing. 'I know you said we shouldn't hope too soon but I can't help feeling wonderfully excited by what you told me. You *do* think it really is a step forward, don't you? Now that we are alone you can be perfectly honest.'

He seemed not to notice his phraseology. He might just as well have said 'now that Molly isn't here!'

She answered him truthfully.

'Yes, I do think it's progress. But only a very, very small step forward, Martin. We've such a long road to go.'

The use of his Christian name came easily and naturally now. Martin was unaware of it but very much aware of the pronoun.

'You said "we", Harriet. I wish I could believe that. You've promised me a year of your life but suppose that isn't long enough?'

Harriet picked nervously at a sliver of wood. Martin was right. It could be years and years before Peter could be called well. Maybe he never would be normal. She was becoming daily more and more deeply involved but without any intention of seeing the job to its conclusion.

'You don't answer!' Martin said. 'And I suppose that is an answer. Well, I won't break my side of the bargain. I said a year—in fact, when we began, I said six months!' He laughed ruefully. 'But I wish to heaven I could make it longer. Oh, hell, I'm not saying what I came out to say which is "thank you". I'm so grateful, and so happy.'

'Oh, please!' Harriet said. 'You know I don't want to be thanked. I'm as thrilled as you are.'

Martin picked up her hand and unconsciously began to brush her palm free of wood splinters.

'One of the things I'm constantly marvelling at,' he said . . . 'is the way you've become so involved with Peter—in just a few weeks. It's hard to believe it isn't longer.'

Harriet nodded. Although Martin seemed satisfied with the cleanliness of her hand, he continued to hold it.

'It would be quite impossible *not* to be involved,' she said gently. 'Apart from Peter's physical beauty, he's so helpless and so lost. I felt it that first day when you brought him here, although I tried to fight it because I really didn't want, in my mind, to become involved. In my heart, I did and I suppose that's how I came to the point of allowing you to persuade me.'

'Then I thank God I kept trying!' Martin said grinning. 'My mother once described me

152

as a revoltingly tenacious child, although naturally she didn't use those words. I used to consider tenacity one of my lesser virtues. Now I'm grateful for it. I hope you won't regret it, Harriet. I haven't wished to pry into something which is no affair of mine, but that young man of yours hasn't been around. I hope you haven't quarrelled because of this?'

Harriet withdrew her hand.

'It wasn't really a quarrel. Justin thought I was being silly to interrupt my career. I wanted to arrange my own life so we disagreed. But we write to each other again now so there's no harm done.'

'And you're still going to marry him?'

Harriet bit her lip.

'I don't know. How can one make up one's mind if you're not sure. I always believed I *would* marry Justin one day, but I don't want to at the moment. I want to live my own life my own way. I want to be absolutely sure when I do get married that I'm really and truly in love. Justin seems to think I should know if I'm in love with him but I don't. How *does* one know?'

Martin sighed.

'I suppose most people would say that if you don't know then you aren't in love. But I'm not the person to ask, Harriet. I don't think I've ever been in love myself.'

Harriet stared at him wide-eyed.

'You weren't in love with your wife?' she

asked astonished.

Martin shrugged.

'Not if being in love produces the reactions described in books and plays and on television. I loved June. I thought we were ideally suited to one another and that we'd be happy together. I was sure I wanted to marry her. And we were happy. But . . . well, to tell you the truth, Harriet, and I've never said this to another living soul, I've sometimes wondered just how much I *did* love her. If it had been all that all-consuming, one-man-one-woman relationship, surely I would not have recovered from her death so quickly and easily? I missed her, desperately at first, but it wore off. I got used to being without her. In a little while, it was almost as if she hadn't existed. Is that all love is—a passing phase in one's life? I don't think so, but I don't know.'

'We're in the same boat then,' Harriet said softly. 'I don't believe my life would virtually come to an end just because Justin wasn't a part of it. Yet I love him. I'd be miserable if I thought I'd never see him again.'

'One could say the same of any very good friend!'

'I know. That's what worries me. Poor Justin!'

Martin laughed.

'Yes, poor Justin. I've no doubt he's crazy about you. It must be hell loving someone who isn't sure she loves you. I never went through

154

that. By the time I got around to loving June, she'd got around to feeling the same way about me. No, the only time I've nearly gone off my head wanting a woman and not sure whether I could get her was when I was trying to persuade you to come and look after Peter! Hardly the same thing, is it? Yet I was in the kind of torment people describe when they are in love. So maybe I do know what it feels like.'

'I have never quite understood why you felt so certain that I was the right person for Peter,' Harriet said, suddenly finding Martin quite easy to talk to on a personal level. Until now they had only communicated about Peter's affairs.

Martin looked at her quizzically.

'That's a point I can't answer logically,' he said. 'But I do know my intuition was right. You *are* good for him. You're calm and restful and easy to be with. Peter must feel this the same way I do.'

'I'm not really a calm or restful person,' Harriet admitted, 'unless I am mentally preoccupied. I get very restive when I'm bored.'

'Then I shall have to see to it you aren't bored,' Martin retorted. 'Are you having enough free time? One evening a week doesn't seem much. Moreover, I understand you spend it with the old doctor and his wife. Don't you want some young company?'

'Not particularly!' Harriet said truthfully.

155

'I've had plenty of that my first year at university. Please don't worry about me. I'm perfectly happy and enjoying my job. If you like, I'll promise to tell you if I begin to feel bored—though I honestly don't see that happening.'

'I would like your promise and thank you for making it. All the same, I'm not going to sit back and take any chances by waiting for the worst to happen. Why don't I take you out for a meal? We could go to the little pub where we lunched—The Fox, isn't it? I'd like to compliment Mr Cooper on his choice of wines and spirits he sent up. What about it, Harriet?'

It was on the tip of Harriet's tongue to agree to the suggestion. It would be nice to get out of the house for a while and away from Molly's brooding gaze. But the thought of Molly brought a return to reason. *She* wouldn't welcome Martin taking her out to dinner, to put it mildly. And in a way, Harriet did not blame her. To be an unwanted third . . .

'I suppose we can scarcely leave poor Molly here on her own,' Martin broke in as if reading her thoughts. 'Dammit, it seemed like such a good idea! There are times when I'm hard put to it to remember all I owe my sister-in-law. She's so impossibly gloomy and touchy these days. She ought not to be living like this. She ought to be leading her own life, finding herself a husband and having a home of her own. Do you know, Harriet, I once tried to suggest to Molly that she did just that and she nearly hit the roof. I simply don't understand her. She's obviously not happy here but she won't leave.'

'She is very fond of you . . . and Peter, of course.'

Martin raised his eyebrows.

'I know that, but it isn't really the right thing for her, is it? After all, there's no future in it for her.'

'Isn't there?' Harriet asked quietly. 'I mean, might there not come a day when you felt you wanted to make the relationship a more personal . . . and permanent one?'

'You don't mean marry her, do you? Good God, Harriet, you can't mean that. I'm fond of Molly naturally, but nothing more. You can't honestly mean you thought I . . .'

'I didn't mean anything at all,' Harriet said quickly. 'Only that your sister-in-law might imagine a future with you rather than without you.'

'I just hope that is as ludicrous a suggestion as the one that I might one day want to marry her. She must know I wouldn't. After all, I met her before I met June. If I'd ever been going to fall in love with Molly, I'd have chosen her then.'

He gave Harriet a long searching look.

'Maybe I'm being very blind,' he said slowly. 'So *you* tell *me*, Harriet, am I missing something right under my nose? Do you think

157

Molly believes I'll propose to her one day? Dammit, do you think she imagines herself in love with me?'

He looked so frightened, Harriet nearly laughed—except that this was no laughing matter as far as Molly was concerned. Pity for her excluded all other emotions and she said lightly:

'How would I know, Martin? You don't imagine your sister-in-law confides in me, do you? She doesn't like me.'

Martin looked relieved. He even laughed.

'For one ghastly moment, I thought you were going to tell me she thought she was in love with me. Conceited, aren't I? Anyway, thank heaven it's not true. Oh, I wish we could just forget all about her and shoot off to The Fox. I feel the need to celebrate. I'm terribly happy, Harriet, and it's all due to you.'

Harriet was once again surprised at how the years dropped away from Martin when he was happy and enthusiastic and on top of the world. He seemed little older than Justin in some ways, or even younger. Justin's nature was always cautious, steady and predictable like his father's. He'd make a good doctor, but he didn't always make for spontaneous fun. Harriet had no doubt that an evening celebration with Martin Blake would be enormous fun. She felt as regretful as he did that they couldn't go.

Fate, however, decreed otherwise. As they

returned to the house, Margaret was in the hall looking for Harriet.

'I've a message from Miss Bradbury,' she said. 'She said to tell you she thinks she's got the 'flu and has gone to bed so she won't be down to supper. Will you be taking yours in the dining-room, Miss Harriet?'

Before Harriet could speak, Martin said:

'No, she won't, Margaret. I thought I'd take Miss Harriet out to dinner for a change and since Miss Bradbury has retired to bed, this would seem an excellent opportunity to go.'

'But what about Peter?' Harriet said. 'I can't leave him.'

'Yes, you can, Miss Harriet. You can safely leave him with me. I won't let him come to no harm, you know that. So off you go and enjoy yourselves.'

Martin gave a boyish whoop of delight but Margaret frowned and nodded towards the landing.

'It wouldn't be wise to disturb Her!' she said enigmatically.

Harriet changed her clothes and this time she dressed with more care than she had on the previous occasion Martin had taken her out for a meal. She wanted to look less ingénue, more sophisticated and appropriate a companion for a man of his age.

Obviously she succeeded in achieving the desired result, for as soon as they had driven away from the house he said:

'You look different, Harriet—older. I'm so used to seeing you in jeans and shirts I'm a bit unnerved by the alteration!'

She knew he was semi-teasing and the mood for the evening was set in a pattern of light-hearted banter. Peter was not mentioned, nor Molly and they devoted their conversation to an exchange of ideas on any topic that happened to arise. Neither was particularly aware of what they ate or drank as they concentrated on the talk.

When Mr Cooper, the landlord, finally called 'Time Gentlemen,' Martin looked at his watch in dismay.

'I don't know where the evening has gone!' he said. 'It has been fun, Harriet, if that's the right word. I'd quite forgotten what it was like.'

His face became suddenly serious.

'I suppose you are well used to evenings like this with your Justin!'

'Oh, no!' Harriet corrected him impulsively. She did not intend any disloyalty to Justin. 'He takes life terribly seriously!'

Martin grinned.

'So do I. Life is a serious business, Harriet. It's just that you haven't discovered its pitfalls yet.'

'Don't be so cynical!' Harriet chided, as Martin paid the bill and helped her to her feet. 'It doesn't become you nearly as well as your other self.'

He walked with her out to the car, his face

once more serious.

'Explain what you mean by my other self,' he said. 'I didn't know there were two of me.'

'Oh, the young and the old you!' Again, Harriet's natural impetuosity led her to voice her opinions before thinking if it was wise to be so frank.

'And you prefer the "young" me, naturally!' Martin said as he switched on the car lights and started the engine. 'I suppose that's very natural seeing you are only a baby by comparison. Well, I like the "old" you—tonight's you.'

They drove out of the village in silence. Martin's mood had suddenly changed from exhilaration to depression. He had enjoyed himself: found himself intensely interested in Harriet and very attracted by her. And that, he told himself, terribly conscious of her nearness in the darkened interior of the car, was probably the understatement of the year. He was quite violently attracted to her. The faint smell of her perfume was far more intoxicating to his senses than the wine they had had with their meal. He even felt a little drunk.

He knew that he could not drive her home without stopping the car to kiss her. He was not sure whether she wanted him to do so but he knew that he would. She had been warm, responsive and apparently as happy all the evening as he. He did not think she would rebuff him—not unless she really were in love

161

with that boyfriend of hers.

He felt a sudden violent spasm of jealousy towards Justin, of his youth, his long years of association with Harriet, his hold over her. What conceit to believe that a girl of Harriet's age would want him, Martin, when she could have a young fellow of her own age.

'Hey, watch it!' Harriet chided him laughing. 'That was a pretty sharp bend you didn't exactly drive round.'

'Sorry!'

Something in that one word caused Harriet to turn her head and regard her companion anxiously.

'Is something wrong?' she asked.

'Why should there be?'

'I don't know. I just felt . . . I don't know . . .'

He pulled the car to a halt and stopped the engine. He did not turn or look at her but leaning his arms on the steering wheel, said:

'When I was growing up there was an older boy in our gang—the leader, I suppose. We all respected him because he was such a howling success with the girls. Naturally we wanted to be like him. Anyway, he once said—and I've never forgotten it. "If you want to kiss a girl, never ask her first if you may do so." I think he was right. And yet . . .'

In the darkness Harriet smiled. For some extraordinary reason, she suddenly felt the older of the two.

'Am I different, then, from other girls?' she

asked softly.

'Yes!' Now Martin did turn. He put one hand beneath her chin and tilted her face so that she was looking directly at him. 'Yes, you are different. Not just young, but different. Harriet, I . . .'

But he broke off and pulled her roughly into his arms, his mouth searching hers in a fierce hunger that frightened Harriet with its intensity. This was not the way Justin kissed. This was not Justin but a man she scarcely knew; with whom she had been mildly flirting all evening yet without any real intention of becoming more closely involved.

Then thought ceased as her body caught fire from his passion and she was swept away in a series of sensations that were new, a little frightening. For the first time in her life, she understood the meaning of sheer physical desire and she found herself with no defence against it.

It was Martin who kept his head and who exerted the necessary control. He released Harriet gently, his fingers softly stroking her hair and tracing their way down her hot cheek to the curve of her lips.

'You're very beautiful!' he said. 'And terribly tempting!' He essayed a smile but it was not easy with Harriet's eyes enormous in her flushed face, regarding him with a mixture of question and appeal.

'Dammit, girl, don't look at me like that!' he

said. 'I'm only human and I want you like hell. Does that shock you?'

She shook her head. Justin had once said the same to her but the words had left her unmoved. Now there was a strong answer inside her body which was reacting in a way she did not understand.

'Darling!' He bent his head and kissed her, softly this time but with a new tenderness. 'I'm trying to remind myself that you are very young and, I believe, very inexperienced. It isn't easy when you look so . . . so appealing.'

'I may be inexperienced but I'm not all *that* young!' Harriet said, regaining her voice. '*I'm* not sorry even if you are!'

Martin pushed her gently back to her side of the car. He pulled out a cigarette case, lit a cigarette and drew on it twice before he said:

'I'm not without experience, Harriet, and one thing I am quite certain about is that the kind of bond, if you can call it that, that exists between us isn't one to be played around with lightly. If you want the truth, I think I frightened you with my desire and I also frightened myself. It was new to me, too—the violence, the passion. Now it has come out into the open we aren't going to be able to ignore it. The fact that neither of us realised it was there before this evening doesn't help now that we do know it. We won't be able to go back to a platonic friendship without thinking, remembering and, as far as I am concerned,

164

wanting.'

Harriet was bringing all her concentration to bear on his words. She understood him. It was as if a new door had opened for her on to a new aspect of life. She could never go back. She did not want to.

'Is it so terrible? That we feel this way?'

His mouth tightened.

'It wouldn't be, if things were different.'

'What things? I don't understand!'

He looked at her then, his eyes miserable and desperate.

'Look, Harriet, when a man and woman feel the way we did just now—the obvious conclusion is that they end up in bed together, either legally, in marriage, or illegally. Neither way is possible for us.'

Harriet flushed.

'I don't see why we should have to start thinking in those kind of terms at . . . at this stage!' she said. 'We've only just met, virtually speaking. We've only kissed once!'

She sounded so young, he nearly weakened, but he knew he must not do so. He cared too much about her.

'Once was quite enough for me to know what you do to me!' he said. 'And I know I couldn't ever feel casual about you, Harriet. I couldn't go for walks holding hands, kiss you in the moonlight, court you, if you like, as if it were all a charming boy and girl idyll that might or might not come to anything. I'm too old for it, Harriet, and you're too innocent for an affair. And even if you weren't, I don't think that's what I'd want, not with you. I know this will sound quite mad to you, but I believe I'm in love with you. Now laugh if you want to.'

But Harriet did not laugh, nor wish to. She was frightened and at the same time, intensely excited. She wanted him to want her. She wanted him to think he was in love with her. For some reason she did not yet understand, it was desperately important that he should care.

'I'm going to take you home,' Martin said as he stubbed out his cigarette. 'Somehow we've got to forget this evening, behave as if it hadn't happened. We're going to be living under the same roof for a hell of a long time and I don't know how it'll work out. But for Peter's sake, we've *got* to go back, not forward.'

He started the car and began to drive home. Harriet felt miserably deflated. She didn't understand what was happening. Martin, for no reason that she could see, had decided to back-track, to pretend that nothing had happened between them. He'd said that he thought he loved her, yet he'd written off marriage or an affair as if either were impossible. Maybe he felt it was far too premature for such kind of commitment. The whole situation seemed to have got quite out of hand. He wanted this evening 'undone' whereas she wanted to hug the memory to her;

to think about it and about her own startling reactions. He fascinated her and attracted her and the very last thing she wanted was to go back to their casual friendship. Why couldn't they let this new relationship develop in its own good time?

Though Martin was partially aware of her confusion, he said nothing to enlighten her. He was feeling angry with himself, even a little angry with her for catching him off-guard. If he had known beforehand what it would be like between them, he'd never have asked her out, or if he had done so, he'd never have stopped the car and kissed her.

But even as one half of his mind said this, he knew with the other half that it wasn't true. He *had* been aware of Harriet before—aware of her femininity and the indefinable sympathy between them. He'd known in his subconscious but had chosen not to recognise it.

Now he would have to pay the price and somehow or other, see that she did not suffer for his selfishness. One thing was certain, he could never marry her. Not just because of the difference in their ages which was surmountable, but because he would not saddle a young girl with a handicapped stepchild. He had no right even to contemplate such a thing. Even if he were to send Peter to an institution which he was loathe to do, he would always remain a liability and no young girl of Harriet's age could be expected to accept it. Moreover, she already had an eligible young man in love with her, anxious to marry her. Harriet would make the perfect wife for a young doctor and he, Martin, had no justification for coming between them even if Harriet were willing. With one half of his mind he ached to know if she reciprocated his feelings to however small a degree. With the other, he realised that if he did not know how she felt, it might prove easier for him to put their relationship back on its old impersonal level. The only thing he did know for certain was that she had been intensely responsive to his kisses and that she must, therefore, have found him attractive. Innocent though she might be, he had recognised in her the same fierce latent passion that was buried deep in his own nature. There could be no milk and water romance between them. If ever they were to make love, it would be all consuming.

Harriet, sitting silently beside him, had no such clarity of thought. She was hopelessly confused. Less than an hour ago, she had been talking and laughing and enjoying a wonderfully carefree companionship with Martin; the more exhilarating because, she now realised, there had been an exciting undercurrent of attraction between them. It had seemed a perfect ending to the evening when Martin had stopped the car and she had known that he was going to kiss her. She'd wanted him to; in fact she would have been bitterly disappointed had he not done so. But somehow it had all swung out of control— touched a deeper undiscovered part of her being which she had only once before experienced with the Welsh boy from the university, and even the strong attraction she had felt towards him was not truly comparative because she had neither known him nor liked him as she did Martin. Martin's kiss evoked not just a physical response but an emotional and mental one as well and she had been totally carried away.

When Martin had said he thought he might be in love with her, she had felt a wave of pure happiness. She wanted him to love her as well as to want her. She relaxed trustingly and in complete content when he held her with such tenderness when the kiss ended. It came as all the greater shock when he seemed suddenly to reject her, pushing her away from him, telling her in so many words that he regretted becoming involved; that since he did not intend to have an affair with her, there could be no future in it for either of them and was best forgotten.

She had felt humiliated, surprised, puzzled, miserably confused. If he had meant that he believed he actually loved her, and he was not merely physically attracted to her, then why could they not get to know one another better? Let their relationship develop slowly or quickly or not at all if that was the way it had to be? Why reject any future for them simply because he felt an affair between them was wrong?

She could only conclude that he had used that word 'love' in the heat of the moment; that what he really meant was that he wanted to make love to her. There was no barrier to love in its other sense. She wasn't engaged to Justin and Martin was a widower and free. He had pleaded the difference in their ages as a reason why they couldn't be like any other couple falling in love, but there was not all that great a disparity and if she did not mind about it, why should he?

She hoped desperately that before they reached the house, he would begin to talk; to explain how he felt. She could not bear it if he were to say a casual 'good-night' as if nothing had happened; or nothing more humiliating than that he thought her too young for an affair and therefore had ceased to be interested in her.

Pride kept her from asking the questions that were beginning to torment her. Deep down inside, she could not believe Martin was the way she had begun to fear he might be. When he had said 'I think I'm falling in love with you!' he had sounded totally sincere and there had been no doubt in her mind as to what he meant by the word 'love'. Perhaps, she thought miserably, she was being incredibly naive and reacting like a romantic little fool.

When Martin turned into the drive, Harriet felt close to tears. She bit hard on her lip and kept her head up, not wishing him to guess how she felt. At least she had not said she thought she was falling in love with him. Such an idea was absurd in any event.

'I don't care what he feels about me!' she thought violently as the car jerked to a halt outside the front door.

She climbed quickly out of the car and opened the door long before Martin could do it for her. She had no intention of waiting for a few crumbs of comfort from anything he might think up to say to cover his odd behaviour.

'It was a lovely evening and a super dinner!' she said brightly, wishing she did not sound like a schoolgirl after an outing. 'Thanks a lot, Martin. It was fun!'

'Harriet . . .'

She pretended she had not heard and with as much dignity as she could muster, she hurried indoors.

Martin stood staring after her, his eyes alone showing his terrible depression. He was astute enough to see through Harriet's over-bright, over-casual behaviour. He could even make a shrewd guess that she was now thinking of him as a middle-aged seducer halted in midstream by a sudden attack of conscience.

He drove the car slowly into the garage, lost in thought. That he had been halted in midstream by an attack of conscience was true enough, but his intention had certainly not been to seduce her. He'd been afraid to let himself fall in love with her and to encourage her to do the same with him.

He parked the car and closed the garage doors. Outside a light rain had begun to fall in keeping with his mood of despair. It was high time he, not Harriet, grew up and faced realities, he told himself wryly. A pretty nineteen-year-old girl was not very likely to fall in love with a middle-aged widower even if that description seemed a little unfair, since he was still in his thirties, and many women had indicated that they found him attractive. Nevertheless, there remained the far greater deterrent than age—his child. What young girl would seriously consider tying herself down to such a handicap? It had been different for Molly—older than Harriet, and a relative of Peter's.

But as Martin walked back to the house, he felt a sudden twinge of uneasiness. Had it really been so easy for Molly? In a way, the fact that she was older than Harriet made it worse, for the longer Molly let the present situation continue, the less likely were her chances of eventual marriage and family of her own. Was it possible that Molly all this time had secretly nursed a hope that *he* would marry her? The thought unnerved him completely. Until now, he had refused to look

172

this possibility squarely in the face, writing it off as ridiculous. Now that he was facing a few facts, the idea that Molly believed herself in love with him seemed horrifyingly possible. It would explain so much—her tireless devotion to Peter; her readiness to cut herself off from society and even to bury herself here in the country alone with him.

There were other pieces of the puzzle sliding into place now that he was ready to look at the picture. Molly's barely concealed jealousy of Harriet! A woman in love often developed an uncanny intuition. Molly might have sensed the attraction Harriet had for him before he had realised it himself.

He went indoors, half-hoping that Harriet might still be about but the house was quiet and he went into the dining-room and poured himself a whisky.

The drink did little to alleviate his fears. He would have liked to ridicule his suspicions about Molly but it was not possible. He knew he would never be completely at ease with her after this. Nor with Harriet. In one evening he had somehow managed to turn his whole world upside down. Yesterday, life had seemed full of hope and promise and he'd been happier these last weeks than he'd felt for years. *Because of Harriet's presence in his home.* He knew that now and by giving way to tonight's impulse, he'd ruined the growing friendship and intimacy between them. She

173

might very well avoid him from now on and he wouldn't blame her. In a way, it would be easier if she did so, yet he knew that it was her company that filled this house with sunshine for him; that it was Harriet he had hurried home to at weekends, leaving the office as early as he could on Friday and staying over till Monday morning.

'*I am* in love with her!' he said, staring into his empty glass and seeing Harriet's image there. 'I want to marry her. I want her in my life all the time, every day, every night. I'm in love for the first time in my life. And I can't tell her. I can't have her.'

A wave of bitterness engulfed him and he sat down at the table and laid his forehead on his arms. All his life he'd worked and fought for what he wanted and most of his desires he'd managed to achieve, if not by acumen then by sheer willpower. Now he wanted something that he had to put out of his reach by voluntary self denial. Because he loved Harriet her future happiness was more important to him than his own.

He permitted himself the luxury of a moment of pure jealousy of the young man, Justin, who could offer Harriet what he could not. Justin had youth and freedom on his side. Martin even permitted himself a few moments of hope; of believing that his little son could be totally cured and cease to be a barrier between himself and the girl he wanted to marry. But he had read enough of Harriet's books on autism now to know that this was so unlikely as to be discounted. Peter might get better but a total cure where he could be called completely normal and no longer require special attention—that would be a miracle and one he had no justification for expecting.

He knew that he could well afford to send Peter away where others could look after him who were paid for their services. But he would never do that unless he knew for a certainty that Peter was beyond knowing or caring where or with whom he was. His child was a part of him, his flesh and blood and he would never desert him for his own selfish desires.

His thoughts turned full circle as he faced the truth for the second time—he had no right to love Harriet or to try to win her love in return. She had given up a year of her life to help his son and for this alone he owed her a great deal. She would never know what it would cost him to keep out of her life; to hide his feelings and pretend indifference. The hardest part of all would be hiding his love. He would liked to have told her; to explain that he knew only too well what it was to be deserted by his father and therefore he could not desert his son! But to do so might be to invite Harriet's pity; and this he did not want. Far better that she should never know.

CHAPTER TEN

When Margaret woke Harriet next morning with an early cup of tea, it was to report that Molly had a temperature of 103 degrees and looked ill enough to need a doctor.

Harriet pulled on a dressing-gown and went along to Molly's room. There was no doubt that Molly was sickening for something and as soon as she had dressed, Harriet reported to Martin that she felt it wise to call in the doctor. He was sitting at the dining-room table, the food Margaret had cooked for him untouched and congealing on the plate. When he heard Harriet come into the room, he quickly picked up the morning paper and tried to steady his racing pulses.

Her words with their impersonal message, made it possible for him to speak as casually as he'd wanted.

'Of course call Dr Barry if you think it necessary,' he said.

Harriet left the room at once and Martin put down the newspaper with a sigh. He had decided during the night to invent some excuse to necessitate his return to London. Now, if Molly were really ill, he could hardly leave as he had hoped. He felt obliged to go up and see Molly and after last night's thoughts about her, he was as reluctant to see her as he was to see

Harriet.

However, he forced himself to pay the required visit. Molly looked flushed and sounded feverish. She essayed a smile as Martin put his head round the door but it was half-hearted.

She had heard Martin's car leave the house before supper and aching and shivering, had sat by the window until the car returned, confirming her painful fear that Harriet had gone with him. Feverish and sick, she had gone back to bed and lain there wondering what she could do. There had to be some way she could discredit Harriet in Martin's eyes, yet nothing she had so far dared to say by way of criticism had had the least effect on him. He had nothing but praise for the girl and the way she handled Peter!

The thought of Peter had dragged her out of bed again. If Harriet had gone out and left the child in a distressed condition, she could bring it to Martin's attention in the morning. But the old servant was sitting by Peter's cot and Molly had had to invent a reason for going into the room, saying she was searching for a thermometer. She thought Margaret looked suspiciously disbelieving but felt too ill and worried to care much what the old woman thought. There was a mutual dislike between them from the start and neither took much trouble to conceal it.

Now, with Martin standing in her doorway

looking awkward and concerned, she could find nothing to say to him that might encourage him to come right into the room, sit down on the chair by her bed and talk to her as if he really cared whether she were ill or not. The thought that he might even hold her hand for a little while was unbearably sweet and she let it sift through her mind while she waited for him to speak.

'The doctor's coming directly after surgery, Molly. Is there anything you want?'

She shook her head, not trusting her voice lest she should break out and say all those words trembling on her lips . . .

'I want you, Martin. I want your arms around me and your head here on the pillow beside me. I want your love. I want to tell you that I'd die for you if you asked me to . . .'

'Has Margaret brought you up any breakfast?'

'I don't want any. I don't want her in here. You know I don't like her!'

Even to herself, she sounded petulant. She saw the quick flick of Martin's eyelids and knew that he was concealing his irritation with her. She felt suddenly vicious.

'Perhaps, if it isn't too much trouble, *you'd* bring me a cup of coffee?'

Martin nodded.

'Of course. I'm sorry you're not well.' He backed out of the doorway and Molly relaxed, waiting for his return. It was almost worth

178

being ill to have Martin wait on her, do something for her.

But it was Harriet who came in with the coffee.

'Martin said you'd like this!' she said, handing her the cup and saucer.

Molly's hatred was so intense she had the greatest difficulty in preventing herself from throwing the scalding liquid in Harriet's face.

'I don't want it!' she said, closing her eyes so that she did not have to see the golden creaminess of Harriet's skin or the soft hair and full red lips that Martin found so fascinating.

Harriet took the coffee away without speaking. Somehow Molly could make just a few words sound ugly and full of hatred. It was impossible to be at ease in her company. There was always this emanation of thinly veiled hatred and jealousy behind Molly's voice. She was a little afraid of what the years of unrequited love had done to this woman. With the reserve and iron self-control, who could say what destruction was being wrought beneath the surface.

Yet uppermost in Harriet's heart as she left the room, was pity, even greater now that she had begun to feel the same hopeless pull of Martin's fascination and her own weakness in the face of it. She had slept hardly at all. When she did so it was to dream that Martin was holding her, kissing her, telling her that he loved her. Waking up had brought tears of disappointment to her eyes. It was only a dream, as unreal as last evening's episode in the car. She would do well to remember it if she did not wish to end up like poor Molly.

Old Dr Barry noticed the shadows under her eyes and remarked on them after he'd seen and left a prescription for the patient.

'Don't *you* go over-doing it,' he said, patting her cheek. 'Let's hope you're not sickening for the 'flu. Heard from Justin recently?'

Harriet remembered with a pang of conscience the letter lying on her desk she had meant and forgotten to answer.

'I'm writing to him today,' she said.

She was shocked to realise that she hadn't given Justin one single thought in the last twenty-four hours. Moreover, she didn't want to think about him. How could she possibly write to him now and say 'I still love you' when she knew only too well that she did not.

She welcomed the distraction afforded her that morning by Peter. Like other autistic children, Peter was content, even happy, to remain in his cot ad infinitum. He would sit or lie or rock in it until someone lifted him out. He had no desires, no needs, no wants. He ate if food was put in his mouth but never asked for it; walked if he was taken for a walk but never explored as other children of his age would wish to do. In so far as he did nothing, he was usually happy but there were occasions

180

which Harriet found intensely challenging when he would suddenly throw a fit of uncontrollable crying.

She had learned that this always occurred if there were some change in the routine of his daily life. Order was necessary to him where speech, knowledge, love, people were not. When he cried, she knew she had to find out why and put the disorder in order for him. It was some hours before she discovered what was wrong with Peter on this occasion. Margaret had brought up his breakfast tray with his cereal in a blue bowl instead of the yellow bowl with a rabbit in the centre which was habitual. The moment she brought up the yellow one, he stopped crying and ate his cereal as usual as she sat spoon-feeding him.

She felt both triumphant and exhausted. Peter, too, was tired and when he crawled over to his cot, she lifted him into it and he promptly fell asleep.

With his usually pale face flushed with crying, his dark hair tousled and unruly, he looked even more like his father than ever. The sight of the small boy lying there made Harriet catch her breath in a sudden helpless rush of tenderness. She sat down by the cot and laid her cool hand on the child's hot cheek. She felt dangerously near to tears. Although she had refused to admit it to herself until now, she had hoped somewhere at the back of her mind that when Martin saw her this morning, he would greet her with some gesture, some sign that last evening in the car had meant something to him too. When he had seemed barely even to notice her, her spirits had taken a downward plunge and had she not been so preoccupied all morning, she would long since have given way to total depression.

She remembered the letter from Justin and in an effort to distract herself now that Peter was asleep and did not need her, she tried to write her reply.

No matter how strongly she willed herself to keep Martin's name off the page, she found it creeping in again and again as she tore up sheet after sheet. It was impossible to write to Justin about her life at Swallow Grange without including the man about whom the house now revolved.

'Martin was so pleased with Peter's progress . . .!'

'Martin took me for a meal at the Fox . . .'

'Martin told me to phone the doctor for Molly . . .' They were all harmless enough sentences and yet she wanted to write to Justin without the one person uppermost in her thoughts being named. Justin was in the middle of exams. She did not want him to guess from her letter how involved she had become. No one must know . . . not Margaret, not Molly and least of all Martin himself.

The letter she finally sealed within its

envelope was jerky and not written with her usual easy style. She hoped Justin would take it for granted that she was as busy as she had stressed.

Margaret knocked on the door and smiling broadly, informed Harriet that since 'She' was in her own room, lunch had been laid in the dining-room for Harriet with Martin.

'Oh, no!' Harriet said, the words coming from her involuntarily. The smile left Margaret's face.

'Now that's a bit strange, Miss Harriet, you not wanting to sit with Mr Blake. Didn't you enjoy yourself last evening?'

Harriet attempted a smile.

'Of course I did. It's just that I'm . . . well, I'm a bit tired and don't feel like making conversation.'

Margaret opened her mouth but closed it again. Harriet knew she was not deceived but the kindly old woman did not pursue the matter.

'I'll move your place into the kitchen, then, alongside of me,' she said.

Harriet felt first relief and then anxiety. She did not want Martin to think she was running away from him—afraid of him. Not to have Sunday lunch with him would be more likely to betray her feelings than if she did so.

'It's all right, Margaret, if you've already laid,' she said. 'I honestly don't mind.'

But it was not easy to be normal with

Martin sitting at the opposite end of the table. She found herself talking too much and too often. She chattered on like some silly schoolgirl about Molly's 'flu, Dr Barry's practice, about Peter and finally about Justin. Martin looked at her fully for the first time.

'When is your young man coming down to see you?' he asked levelly. He saw the colour rush to her cheeks and wished he'd never asked the question. Now he was wondering jealously if the boy did mean more to her than he had supposed.

'He's in the middle of exams,' Harriet said for the second time. 'I don't expect to see him until the summer vacation.'

'We must arrange for you to have plenty of time off then, so you can see something of each other!' Martin heard himself saying.

Harriet protested at once.

'I've a job to do and Justin understands that.'

Martin nodded and resumed his eating. The whole situation was proving far more difficult even than he had imagined. Since there was nothing more seriously wrong with Molly than a bout of 'flu, he decided he'd return to London that afternoon.

'I've a conference first thing on Monday morning,' he lied to Harriet as Margaret served the sweet course. 'So I'll be driving back around tea-time.'

Harriet kept her eyes on her plate. Her

184

disappointment was total. So long as Martin was here in the house, he might say something to indicate that he really did care about her. He was so distant it was as if there was a layer of ice between them; a barrier she was increasingly sure he meant to erect to keep her from showing her feelings. It was as if he guessed that she'd fallen in love with him and wanted her to understand at once that there was no future in it. Yet it had been he who had said 'I think I'm falling in love!' Nothing made sense any more.

She spent the afternoon taking Peter for a walk, half hoping, half dreading that Martin would leave whilst she was out. But he was waiting in the hall when she and the boy returned.

'I wanted to say goodbye to Peter!' Martin said as if there had been a need to excuse the hour he chose to leave.

He picked the boy up and kissed him gently. As usual there was no response from Peter but unusually, Martin commented on it, his voice hurt and bitter.

'If only he'd put his arms round me and hug me,' he said. 'Just once!'

Across the child's head, his eyes met Harriet's and she saw the pain of the boy's rejection in them and forgot her resolve.

'You mustn't give up hope,' she said. 'I believe he will one day. Honestly, Martin, I do believe it and you must, too.'

185

He stood there looking at her for a full minute. Then he said:

'If you believe it, I will, Harriet . . .'

He took a step towards her and for one moment she thought he was going to put his arms round her. But no sooner did he raise them than he let them drop once more to his sides. His eyes turned away from her. He murmured something about collecting his suitcases and then walked off without a backward glance.

Harriet stood perfectly still, staring after him. For a brief space of time she remained there, feeling as if a ton of lead had been lifted from her shoulders. Martin did care. She knew it. He may not have touched her, kissed her, said no more than her name yet she knew it. Then the certainty began to fade like a mirage and the radiance left her eyes as doubt began to creep in once more. It could all be wishful thinking. Because she wanted him to give some indication however tiny, she had let herself build up hope on one word, her name and the tone of voice he'd used as he had spoken it.

'I'm going mad!' Harriet told herself severely. 'And the sooner I stop imagining things the better!'

But she could not write off as imagination the terrible feeling of emptiness and loneliness that engulfed her as she heard Martin's car disappear down the drive.

For two days she see-sawed from hope to despair. She nursed Molly, threw herself into renewed care and effort with Peter, filled the hours of the day as full as she could. But at night, the miserable mental turmoil returned as she tried to believe that Martin's kiss, his words, his sudden departure to London all indicated that he did love her; only to be succeeded by disbelief as day succeeded day without a letter, a phone call or even a promise that he would be home for the weekend to reassure her.

Martin did not come home that next weekend, the first one he had missed since moving into the house. Molly received the news from his secretary, a brief telephone message which she passed on to Harriet. Her face was chalk white and the skin of her cheekbones seemed to Harriet to be stretched taut as the after effects of 'flu and her present anger and disappointment were all too clearly revealed.

'He's not coming back and it's all your fault!' Molly said, pointing a trembling finger at Harriet who had just taken her lunch on a tray to her bedroom. 'And don't pretend you don't know what I'm talking about. I can see through you, my girl. I know your sort. You don't want him yourself but you don't want anyone else to have him either!'

The low hiss of Molly's voice was more venomous and frightening than a shout would have been. Harriet stared at her aghast.

'I really *don't* know what you're talking about!' she said truthfully.

'Oh, yes, you do! I know you went out with him last weekend. I saw you with my own eyes. You've been very clever, Miss Smarty, from the word go, playing on Martin's sympathy, getting all you could out of him, making a right fool of him and then giving him the cold shoulder when he wanted something in return. I could have warned him. Anyone could see what you were up to, pretending it was Peter you were interested in when all the time you just wanted Martin's money.'

Harriet gasped. She was finding it hard to credit that Molly really meant what she was saying. She sounded delirious and yet Harriet knew Molly had no temperature now and was convalescing.

'You're not well!' she said as soothingly as she could. 'You don't mean what you've been saying. It's too ridiculous.'

Molly's face twisted in a sneer.

'Is it?' The voice was cold and cruel. 'Are you trying to tell me that Martin doesn't give a damn about you? He's crazy about you and you know it.'

Harriet's cheeks flamed, not with guilt as Molly supposed, but with a sudden revival of hope. If Molly was this jealous, maybe she was right and Martin did care after all!

'There, you can't hide the truth from me!'

Molly said triumphantly. 'Well, I can tell you one thing, Madam, you won't get one dollar more out of him if I can help it. I'll make him see what you're up to and when he understands what a sucker you're making of him, he'll send you packing. I can take care of Peter, I always have until you came!'

Harriet could have defended herself, argued that Molly had the picture all wrong; that far from trying to attract Martin so she could extort money from him (the thought was ludicrous) she was desperately attracted by him and wanted nothing more from him than some sign that he cared about her. But she would not lower herself to defend herself against the ravings of a woman who must surely be mentally sick.

She left the room and went along to the nursery. Peter was where she had left him, piling bricks in neat rows by the window. She went over and sat down beside him, needing the comfort of his warm little body even though she knew there could be no comfort from his emotional responses. She hugged him and he made no move to evade her embrace. Feeling calmer, she reached in her pocket and brought out a packet of sweets she kept there for him, and put one in his mouth. Quite suddenly, he reached out his hand, removed a sweet from the paper packet and turning to her, put it in her mouth.

Somehow Harriet managed to contain her

excitement. In this one simple little gesture she recognised a huge step forward—Peter had of his own free will made contact with her, with another human being. He had recognised her existence. For an autistic child it was progress far out of proportion to the simple gesture involved. Deliberately, she gave no sign of noticing anything different in his behaviour and he returned at once to his bricks and did not approach her in any way again that day.

Harriet longed to rush to the telephone to give Martin the news but she did not do so, afraid lest he should think she was using Peter as an excuse to bring him home at the weekend. If he telephoned her for news, she would, of course, tell him. But he did not phone and the week passed without further event.

As if aware that she had said far too much, Molly did not address another word to Harriet. Although she got up and dressed, Molly stayed in her own bedroom and ordered Margaret to bring all her meals up there.

Harriet anticipated a quiet weekend but it was not to be. On the Friday evening Dr Barry telephoned to tell her that Justin was flying down from Scotland for a few days mid-term holiday and wanted her to go over for dinner.

Glad of an excuse, Harriet explained that with Molly still not completely fit and Martin away, she did not feel she should leave the house.

'In that case Justin will come round and see you!' Dr Barry said cheerfully, unaware that this was the last thing Harriet wanted.

She knew now, beyond any doubt, that she could not marry Justin; that if she could feel as she did about Martin, she could not possibly be in love with Justin. She dreaded the hurting of Justin's feelings, of having to tell him she had fallen in love with Martin! Now he was coming to see her, he would be bound to guess something was very wrong. He would demand an explanation and she owed him the truth. It made no difference that Martin was not in love with her. The important thing as far as Justin was concerned was that she did not love him the way he wanted; the way she should love the man she intended to marry.

Her misgivings about the impending visit from Justin were off-set by yet another encouraging moment with Peter. Some weeks earlier she had bought the very simplest of jigsaw puzzles, a set of six wooden shapes which put together showed a pony very like Knackers, on whom Peter clearly enjoyed riding every day. He had shown no interest in the puzzle until this Saturday morning. Harriet was sitting beside him on a rug in the garden, her mind on Justin, her fingers idly fitting pieces of the puzzle together. Suddenly, Peter reached out a hand and put a section in place, correctly. Harriet paused, waiting for him to repeat the action but he must have sensed her

191

excitement, for the next time he did not use his own hand but used hers to touch the pony's head and lift it into place. They played like this until the puzzle was complete and then Peter seemed to retract into himself again; behaving as if she were not there. Yet she was quite sure he was aware of her presence.

That evening at bedtime, Peter waited for her to turn on the bath taps. He always enjoyed water and no matter how fractious his mood during the day, bath-time seemed to calm him. Harriet, sensing his impatience, suddenly decided to delay the action of turning the taps to see what he would do. For several moments, he stood quite still whimpering in the odd way he had. Then, as she held her breath waiting, he reached out to take her hand and propelled it towards the taps. Obediently she turned one on, then let her hand fall limp again. Once again he lifted her hand to the second tap. This time, Harriet gently slid her fingers out from beneath his and laid her hand on top so that he was the one turning the tap rather than she. He showed great excitement as if aware of this new achievement and Harriet realised that this was yet another step forward. However minute the steps, Peter was beginning to move out of his world into the real one where other people and other things existed. He could no longer be said to be totally beyond recall and to have reached this point in so few weeks was progress indeed!

When Peter was tucked up in bed and nearly asleep, Harriet went down to the kitchen to talk to Margaret whilst she waited for Justin to arrive. Margaret did not understand Peter's illness but she was fond of the little boy and delighted to hear from Harriet that everything was going so well.

'And I'm that pleased for Mr Blake, too,' Margaret added. 'Poor man, he hasn't had much happiness in his life, has he? For all his wealth!'

Before Harriet could reply, Justin walked into the kitchen. He looked brown and fit and very handsome. Harriet found herself staring at him as if he were a stranger she was seeing for the first time. It was easy, seeing him standing there smiling at her, to imagine a girl falling in love with this attractive young man. If only . . . if only *she* could have loved him.

'Harry darling, you look tired but beautiful. How are you? And how's my best girl?' he added with a grin as he walked over to Margaret and gave her a kiss on the cheek.

'None the better for you messing me about whilst I'm trying to cook supper. Away with you, Mr Justin, and you, Miss Harriet, and leave me in peace.'

Justin laughed and pulled Harriet out of her chair.

'Come on, let's have a drink in the garden,' he said. 'Dad said the Boss Man was away so I presume we can do as we please.'

Still silent, Harriet found glasses and filled them and took Justin out to the terrace where there were chairs and a table overlooking the lawns. Justin sat down with a sigh of contentment.

'I always forget how lovely this house and garden are,' he said. 'And you, Harry. Seems ages since I saw you.'

'It does to me, too!' Harriet said. 'Though I didn't expect to see you till the summer vacation. Is this trip home for any special reason, Justin?'

The smile left his face and he looked down at his glass with a slight frown.

'As a matter of fact it is!' he said. 'I wanted to see you, Harry. That last letter of yours . . .' he looked up and gave her a wry grin. 'Well, it wasn't what you did say but what you didn't say, darling. Maybe I'm reading wrong things between the lines but it did seem to me that you'd finally fallen out of love with me. Am I wrong?'

It was a straight question and Harriet knew that she could not lie. At the same time, she could not find the right words to express her sadness, her regret, or what she did feel for him.

Justin broke her silence.

'Don't look so miserable about it, Harry. I suppose I've known for a long time. I just did not want to accept it. The fact is, I don't think

194

you were ever really in love with me the way I was with you.'

'I thought I was. I honestly did, Justin.'

He reached out and covered her hand with his.

'Don't look so tragic, darling. It's not the end of the world! I suppose in my heart of hearts I always knew you'd never marry me. It was a dream, wasn't it? One we both grew up with and took for granted. I think I'll always love you, no matter what.'

'Oh, Justin!' Harriet said helplessly. 'I wish I could make that dream come true—for both of us. But I can't . . . I can't . . .'

'I know luv! I also know that if I hadn't come down here and told you, you'd never have plucked up courage to tell me. I came to the conclusion that it would be best all round if I called it a day and I wanted to be quite sure before I did so.'

'Justin, we won't stop being friends?' He smiled reassuringly.

'Of *course* not, silly. In a way, nothing is going to be any different than it always was— except that we won't be planning to get married to each other. I can't quite envisage it at the moment, but I don't doubt a few years from now, I'll be married to some other girl and you'll be Mrs Someone Else and we'll be happily nostalgic about our youthful past and insist on our unwilling children being the best of friends!'

Harriet smiled. Justin was making it wonderfully easy for her.

'Do you have anyone in mind?' she asked.

'Oh, there are one or two girls chomping at the bit at university!' he said. 'I haven't followed up the invitations as yet but I dare say I will now. But what about you? Was I wrong in thinking you were beginning to fall in love with Martin Blake?'

Harriet's blush contradicted her denial.

'Why should you think so?' she prevaricated.

'Just because you used to talk about him such a lot and these last few letters—not a word. It was as if you were afraid you'd say too much. Are you in love? Isn't he rather old for you? What's he really like?'

From that moment on, there was no further restraint between them. It was as if the years had rolled away and they were children again confiding their secrets and hopes and fears to each other. Margaret called them in to supper but they were too busy talking to notice what they were eating and before long they were once more out in the garden and Justin was saying:

'Since you ask me, Harry, I'd say the poor man is as much in love with you as you are with him. If he's not he must be out of his mind. You know, luv, you've changed quite a bit since I last saw you. You've blossomed out, as they say! And into a very beautiful young woman. No wonder Blake ran away.'

'But why?' Harriet said. 'We had no quarrel. As I told you, everything was wonderful.'

'I imagine he was taken by surprise and wanted time to think about it before he became too deeply involved. People always do have reasons for their odd behaviour, however obscure. Maybe he has promised to marry the wretched Molly and doesn't know how to extricate himself. I really don't like the idea of you being alone in this house with that woman, Harry. She sounds quite mental.'

Harriet sighed. She could not feel anything but pity for Martin's sister-in-law. Perhaps Justin was right and Martin was far more deeply committed to Molly than he had let her suppose.

Justin put an arm round Harriet's shoulder and gave her a warm hug.

'Don't look so despairing. It'll all come right, you'll see.' He sounded so reassuring and at the same time, affectionate and caring, she turned instinctively towards him and hugged him back.

'I'll always love you, too, Justin,' she said. She had been about to add that all her old affection for him had returned in full now that they were just friends again, but before she could say more, a voice said from a window above them:

'Very touching. I'm sure Martin will be most interested to hear how you carry on when he isn't here, Harriet.'

Justin jumped up and turned towards the window but Molly had slammed it shut. Angrily, he said:

'That woman is vicious, Harry. Dangerous! She'll tell Blake I was here and no doubt she'll give him a distorted version of what we've been saying to each other. I wonder just how much she did hear?'

'I don't care!' Harriet said defiantly. 'I'm not ashamed if she heard me say I was in love with Martin.'

Justin remained silent. He was unhappily aware that at the moment Molly chose to listen, Harry had not been expressing love for Martin Blake, but for him, even if she hadn't intended the same kind of love.

If it weren't for Peter, I'd insist you came home with me,' he said thoughtfully. 'I really don't trust her, Harriet. She's not normal.'

Harriet shrugged.

'Margaret's here in the house. I'll be all right, Justin. All the same, I think you'd better leave now. Will you come round tomorrow?'

'You know I will, Harry. Be a good girl and lock your door, just to please me, will you?'

She gave him her promise and after kissing her a brief good night, Justin walked off in the direction of home.

As Harriet went back into the house she heard the faint tinkle of the telephone bell. She was certain that Molly must have been speaking on it on the upstairs extension. Margaret never used the instrument and there was no one else who would. It was not difficult to guess Molly had been phoning Martin.

Harriet's guess was right.

In the flat in London, Martin replaced the receiver and white-faced, went back to the silent emptiness of the sitting-room. He had been pacing the room restlessly most of the day, trying to fight against the terrible temptation to get in his car and drive to Swallow Grange; to Harriet. He had no doubts left that he loved her. He had argued with himself all afternoon and evening as to whether, after all, he could ask her to marry him. Reason told him he had no right, but his emotions clamoured for a release from his conscience. Harriet knew far better than most women what the problem of Peter entailed. If he asked her to marry him she could refuse. Why should he take her refusal as a foregone conclusion? Even if it were likely, he had at least a glimmer of hope.

That hope, however, was ruthlessly dashed when Molly phoned him. Her call had been unexpected and quite shattering. He'd forgotten Justin and had certainly not expected him to be at Swallow Grange the one weekend he was away.

Martin sat down on the settee and lit a cigarette with hands that were shaking. Molly had not minced words. According to her, she had surprised Harriet with 'her young man, carrying on in the garden'. The implication had been of the worst and Martin's imagination had supplied the details Molly omitted. He knew only too well what it was like to kiss Harriet, hold her, want her; he knew, too, how warmly and passionately she responded. It sickened him to think that only three nights after he had kissed her in his car, she was now in the embrace of another man. His hands shook with humiliation and jealousy.

'You've got to get rid of her!' Molly had said. 'The girl's a slut, Martin, and you've been too blind to see her for what she is . . . trying to seduce you because she knows you've got money . . . acting the little innocent . . . pretending she really cares about Peter . . .'

Molly had gone on and on until he had shut his ears against the tirade, sickened and hurt and miserably afraid lest she was telling the truth. Not even Molly could make up such lies, he told himself wretchedly.

Or could she? If the saying were true that 'hell hath no fury like a woman scorned', then indeed he had scorned Molly and if he let himself believe Harriet was as she described, her revenge in this form was total.

Martin found himself recalling past occasions when he had feared that Molly might be in love with him. He thought of the strange hatred of Harriet Molly had not troubled to hide, even before she had known Harriet well enough to form a judgement about her. Molly's devotion to Peter could have been a means to an end, just as she had implied Harriet had only pretended an interest in his son. That much he knew to be a lie. Harriet had thrown up her university career to help the boy and no one would ever convince Martin she was not genuine in her interest in Peter. He'd seen her too often with his own eyes, gentle, tender, caring. And when he thought about it, he'd never once seen Molly in similar acts of love, even in the old days when she had care of him. Could it be that Molly had used the boy for her own ends? Clinging to Peter when it might have been better for him to be in more experienced hands, simply in order to cling to him, Martin?

Yet try as he might, Martin could not engender any real belief in Molly's duplicity. He'd known her, trusted her, too long to think badly of her—or as badly as all that. At the same time he did believe she was capable of lying and she could have been lying about Harriet and Justin. And he'd have no peace until he knew. If Harriet was in love with Justin and meant to marry him, the sooner he found out for certain the better it would be for him. In his present frame of mind, he could not work, could not sleep, eat, enjoy himself. If this was love, then he longed to be out of love, for there was no peace in it—only torment.

Martin stubbed out his cigarette and reached in his pocket for his car keys. Late though it now was, he was going to drive home to Swallow Grange.

'Home!' he echoed his own thought as he climbed into his car. So that was how he thought of Harriet's house! Home was the place where the woman you loved lived. If he could only believe that Harriet would be there with open arms and shining eyes— waiting for him.

CHAPTER ELEVEN

Molly sat on the edge of her bed, her hands clasped together to stop them trembling. She was shaking with an intense internal excitement, the more hysterical because she was determined to give no outward sign of it. The laughter that might have echoed through the sleeping household remained deep inside her like the children she had never borne; like the love she had never expressed. She was well trained in the art of repression and now, only the quivering hands and the nervous flick of her eyelids betrayed her tension.

She had given Martin a very nasty shock. She knew that because, totally unlike him, he had not argued or questioned but had stayed silent. She'd not been mistaken in thinking he was falling in love with Harriet—silly little Harriet who had played very nicely into her hands. She'd wanted for weeks to discredit her but Harriet had given her no chance to do so and Molly had not dared to fabricate too improbable a lie lest Martin should see through it and turn against *her*. Now even that bad-tempered servant, Margaret, could not deny that Justin was here this evening and that they had sat out in the garden together, kissing and talking about love! Martin might well be jealous! She'd made it plain enough over the telephone that she thought he ought to come home and do some checking up on Harriet himself. Molly had pointed out that Harriet was probably badly neglecting Peter whilst she was carrying on with her boy friend!

If things went the way she, Molly, planned, Harriet would be sent packing before long and she, herself, would take over Peter again and thereby re-establish contact with Martin. Since they'd been in this house, he's barely had time for her now there was no Peter to talk about.

Peter! Molly's fingers gripped more tightly into her palms. The boy was one certain sure way to Martin's heart. If she could only prove, somehow, that Harriet was harming him, Martin would not hesitate to send her away. If only . . .

Her head was aching. For a moment, the thundering inside her skull prohibited coherent thought. But gradually the noise stopped and her brain seemed icy cold and astonishingly clear. If Harriet would not harm the boy, she, Molly, would. The blame would be laid at Harriet's door, not hers.

She smiled at the brilliance of her deductions. It seemed strange that she had not thought of it before. She did not have to do anything very terrible—only make it appear as if Harriet had neglected her charge in some unforgivable way. She need not hurt him physically.

The tension became too much for her. She jumped up and began to pace the room, to and fro, to and fro, while she enlarged on her scheme. There was the pony Harriet seemed to think was so good for Peter. If it could be made to bolt! Yet she knew this was practically impossible since the pony was too old to trot let alone gallop and even if it were to do so, Peter might be killed. There was the lake, forbidden as a place to take the boy as water held a fascination for him and it was feared he might wander down there by himself if he knew of its existence. But then Martin might not believe her if she implied that Harriet had taken the boy there since she had been the one to say it could be dangerous. Besides, the boy might have wandered down on his own, not realising water was there until he came upon it, and that would not imply carelessness on Harriet's part.

Molly's feverish brain twisted and turned. It

fell finally upon the attic. Peter was in no danger from ordinary stairs since he lacked any sense of adventure and made no move, even if left on the upstairs landing, to walk or crawl down them. But if he were found in the attic! The only descent was by a steep ladder which the boy could not possibly negotiate safely since he had no strength in the disused muscles of his small hands. Harriet might have dumped him there when she had wanted to go off to meet Justin. Peter could never climb up there by himself so Martin would have to accept that someone had put him up there, and who else but Harriet had a motive? Certainly not the old servant who never went near the child except to take him his meals and clean the rooms. As for himself, she would return to bed with a recurrence of the 'flu from which she had barely recovered, so she would not be suspected. Harriet would have to take the blame.

Some of the tension began to ease as her plans became clearer. She lay down on the bed, closing her eyes and allowing her mind to drift. It dwelt crazily and contentedly on the certain consequences. She could imagine the look of horror and surprise on Harriet's pretty little face when she was accused by Martin of neglect of her duty and told to go! She could imagine Harriet's protests and Martin's stern, unrelenting face as he told her she might well have been responsible for Peter's death if he had fallen down the ladder. Martin would give her no quarter. Shocked at the outcome of his stupid experiment with a young girl, he would turn to her, Molly, for help. He would, once more, rely on her, depend on her; perhaps once his stupid infatuation for Harriet was squashed, he would realise that it was her, Molly, he had really loved all the time.

Only one small item remained to be resolved—when Peter should be put in the attic. Not until Martin was back. Her instinct told her he would not stay away long—not now he knew Justin Barry was here making love to the girl he, Martin, wanted.

Exhausted though she was, Molly's tortured brain would not allow her to sleep this night as on any other night. As was now her custom, she got up and took two sleeping pills. They were strong ones she had stock-piled when she was in London, knowing she might one day need a stronger dose than she had at that time. Now even two pills took over-long to act. But finally the drug quietened her and when Martin's car turned into the drive she, like Harriet, was deeply asleep.

*   *   *

Despite the drug she had taken, Molly woke early. The sleep had not refreshed her and she felt sick, breathless and heavy-headed. Only her brain seemed alive and it required an effort of will to force her body to the physical effort of getting up and going to her window to try to revive herself in the fresh morning air.

Breathing deeply with her eyes closed, she did not at first see Martin's car, standing outside the front door. When she did so, her heart began to pound, intensifying the pain in her head.

So he was back! Now, far sooner than she had anticipated, she could put her plan into action.

Alert now, she looked at her watch. It was only six-thirty. Not even Margaret would be awake. She could go to Peter's room, carry the boy up to the attic and return unseen by anyone. Later, when Harriet woke and found Peter not in his cot, the household would waken and in her own good time she, Molly, would inform Martin that she had seen Harriet slipping out of the house late last night, to go and meet Justin.

Molly smiled. It was all so easy—as if at long last a kindly Fate was working to her ends; to bring her Martin's love. For so long now Martin had kept her in torment, using her, neglecting her, hurting her by his indifference, yet implying hope by his very dependence on her. She hated him as well as loved him. Now she had him in her power. It would be good to see him suffer; to watch him send out of his life the girl he thought he loved; to see him regret he had ever entrusted his son to the care of an immoral young girl. She would make all her predictions about Harriet come true.

Without stopping to dress, clad only in a thin nylon nightdress, barefooted, Molly opened her bedroom door. The house was silent. Quietly she walked along the carpeted corridor, pausing outside Harriet's door to listen. There was no sound. Smiling, Molly moved to the next door—Peter's. It opened without noise and she left it unclosed as she walked over to the cot. The boy was curled up like an embryo, only his dark curly head, breathtakingly like Martin's, showing above the pale blue blanket.

She felt a weakness in her legs. For a moment she forgot why she was here, over-come with a longing to take the boy in her arms and hold him, hold that dark head to her breast. It was so long since she had done so and been almost happy believing it to be Martin in her arms.

Her head was throbbing again. She was uncertain what to do next. Desperately, she tried to think calmly what she had come to do. Then she remembered. She bent and lifted the boy, still nestling in the warmth of the blanket.

His eyes opened but he seemed not to see her. He lay passively but heavily in her arms. She had not realised how much weight he had put on nor how heavy he would be to carry. She gasped, fighting for breath, her legs trembling.

Willpower overcame inertia; she straightened up and managed to carry her burden through the doorway. The long landing looked even longer as she stared down its length, to the door of the boxroom from which the ladder rose to the attic. Then she had her first doubt that she would be able to get there, let alone carry the boy up the ladder. She was far weaker than she had thought although she knew she had lost a great deal of weight lately.

Breathing deeply and unevenly, she staggered along the carpeted landing. By the time she reached the boxroom door, she was trembling violently and the supreme effort of opening the door still carrying the boy, was too much for her. She half fell into the room and Peter, awake now, began to whimper. Quickly, angrily, fearfully, she pushed the door shut and put her hand over the boy's mouth. Then she sat down beside him, shaking her head from side to side. She had once more forgotten what it was she intended to do.

She looked round the unfamiliar room, wondering where she was. The boy struggled free and began to scream. Some last remaining vestige of sanity told Molly that she had to stop the boy making so much noise. She grabbed him and once again her hand covered his mouth.

She was not aware of how long she sat there. Time no longer had any meaning. She felt very, very tired but though she would have liked to sleep, she did not relax her hold on Peter. When Martin found her, he had to use every ounce of his strength to prise her hands away from the boy's mouth. His face was ashen with shock and fear. Harriet, who had followed close behind him, said urgently:

'Don't shout at her, Martin. She's ill!'

The fury on Martin's face slowly died out as Harriet stooped to lift the gasping child into her arms. He began to recover his breath and Martin realised that no matter what evil intentions Molly had had, she had not harmed the boy.

Shaken and appalled, he looked down at Molly. She smiled up at him innocently.

'You came home, Martin!' she said. 'I've waited so long. Don't go away again! I need you.'

Martin felt momentarily sick. He did not want to touch her but he forced himself to raise her gently to her feet. Beside him, Harriet said:

'Put her to bed. I'll phone Dr Barry. She's very ill.'

Martin nodded speechlessly.

'Peter's all right!' Harriet said reassuringly. 'I'll put him back in his cot. There's nothing to worry about, Martin, only . . .'

She glanced down at Molly and bit her lip. There was a look of vacant stupidity on Molly's face. She seemed quite unaware now

210

of their presence in the room and was mumbling to herself, her eyes closed.

As Martin began to guide her slowly along the landing towards her room, he found himself listening to Molly's rambling and began to make sense of what she was saying. It seemed she had been trying to take Peter up to the attic—not to harm him but with the intention of proving to him, Martin, that Harriet was irresponsible and dangerous for Peter. In her distorted brain, she believed she had achieved her plan to discredit Harriet for as Martin laid her on the bed and pulled the eiderdown over her, she smiled up at him and said:

'Harriet will have to go away, won't she, Martin? I'll look after Peter for you and we'll just be the three of us—the way it used to be.'

Martin turned away quickly. He realised that Molly had had some kind of breakdown and was not responsible. He hoped for all their sakes that the doctor would send her away to hospital because if the doctor did not, he himself could not let her remain under his roof any longer. He should have sent her away years ago but he'd been too blind to see through her façade. He felt both guilty and ashamed of his neglect.

'You mustn't blame yourself, Martin,' Harriet said later when they sat downstairs waiting for the doctor to come. 'You say you were too blind to see she was in love with you, but I would say you were too modest. A more conceited man might have jumped to the right conclusions ages ago.'

Martin looked up and felt his heart jump. Despite her pallor, Harriet looked very beautiful and strangely mature although she was wearing what must have been a school dressing gown over equally child-like pyjamas. He reminded himself she was only nineteen— far, far too young to consider marriage to a thirty-two-year-old widower, but his willpower seemed to have deserted him completely for he heard himself say:

'I've fallen in love with you, Harriet. I know this isn't the time to be telling you but it's the truth and there doesn't seem to be any point in pretending now.'

Harriet stared back at him, her heart racing. A wonderful warm happiness overwhelmed her so that she could not speak. 'I realise there's very little hope you might ever want to marry me,' Martin continued. 'For all I know, you may be thinking of marrying your young medical student and if you are, I . . .'

'I told Justin I'd never marry him when he came to see me last evening,' Harriet broke in softly. 'You see, Martin, I found out I didn't love him. I knew it when I fell in love with you.'

A look of bewilderment swept Martin's face.

'But Molly said . . . no, I don't think I ever did believe what she said when she telephoned me last night. At first, I was jealous, horribly so. Then I knew she couldn't be speaking the truth. Yet I had to come here, see you, find out if you were in love with the boy. Oh, Harriet, can I really believe what you said just now—that you love me?'

'Well, for goodness sakes, Miss Harriet, say "yes" and have done with it!' Margaret's voice spoke from behind them. She had come in with a tray of tea and neither had heard her. She looked at their startled faces and gave a mischievous wink.

'Doctor will be coming any minute!' she added.

Harriet's face broke into a smile. She jumped up and put an arm round the old woman, hugging her.

'How did you know?' she said. 'I tried so hard not to show it.'

'Isn't no mistaking love, Miss Harriet. I could see it coming to the both of you for some time—before you knew it yourselves. I'm right, aren't I, Mr Martin?'

Martin, too, stood up. He went to Harriet, putting his arm round her and holding her against him. His face was very serious, without the radiance that shone on Harriet's. 'You're both forgetting Peter!' he said softly. 'I've thought so much about it and I can't believe I have the right to ask you to take on a child like my son when you're barely past being a child yourself. I'm right, aren't I, Margaret? No

213

matter how much I love Harriet, I can't ask her to marry me.'

Harriet did not wait for Margaret's reply. Throwing her arms round Martin, she said breathlessly:

'But I want Peter, too, Martin. Even if it weren't for you, I'd never leave Peter now. I haven't had a chance to tell you yet but there's been some wonderful progress. Martin, yesterday . . .'

'There's the bell. That'll be Doctor!' Margaret broke in.

Martin's eyes held a look of sheer joy as he said smiling:

'You must tell me about it later, darling. First, we must see about poor Molly.'

For a little while, until the ambulance came to take Molly to hospital, out of their lives and into a calmer, peaceful world where she could recover, they hoped, in time, they could not think of themselves or the future. When she had gone, the doctor with her, they were alone once more, sitting side by side, hands clasped as Harriet told Martin that she had no doubts now that his little boy would eventually get better.

'We'll make him well again—between us,' she said, her face glowing with enthusiasm and excitement. 'Don't you see, Martin, he's bound to get well now with both of us wanting him, loving him, helping him. I'll give up university and we'll . . .'

'No, darling, you won't!' Martin said gently. 'Much as I want to have you to myself every moment of every day for the rest of my life, I'm not going to be selfish. We'll find somewhere for Peter to go where he'll get specialised help while you go back to school and finish your training. It's what I want. You're going to be a wonderful psychologist and I'm not going to be responsible for ruining your career.'

Harriet smiled a small secret smile. As if that ambition had any meaning now! All she wanted was to marry Martin as soon as ever it was possible and spend her life loving and caring for him and Peter. But they need not argue about it now. Even if Martin was right and she owed it to him as well as to herself to complete her training, that decision could wait. 'Do you realise you haven't kissed me?' she said softly. 'Not since we were in your car.'

He nodded, his eyes filled with love as he bent his head and put his lips longingly to hers.